THE LAST DAYS OF SALTON ACADEMY

JENNIFER BROZEK

RAGNAROK
PUBLICATIONS

CRESTVIEW HILLS, KENTUCKY

THE LAST DAYS OF SALTON ACADEMY
Ragnarok Publications | www.ragnarokpub.com
Editor In Chief: Tim Marquitz | Publisher: J.M. Martin
The Last Days of Salton Academy is copyright © 2016 by Jennifer Brozek.
All rights reserved.

Published by Ragnarok Publications, LLC
206 College Park Drive, Ste. 1
Crestview Hills, KY 41017

ISBN-13: 9781941987704
Worldwide Rights
Created in the United States of America

Editor: Tim Marquitz
Associate Publisher: Melanie R. Meadors
Publishers Assistant: Gwendolyn Nix
Graphic Design Coordinator: Shawn T. King
Cover: M.S. Corley

Acknowledgments

Thank you to Jeff for agreeing to be my bad guy and to all of my friends loosely modeled in this story. Just remember, if I murder you horribly in a story, it means I like you.

"The Salton Academy is a preparatory school for boys and girls. Education, manners, and training are key. Here, we plan for excellence, we plan for success, and we plan for the future so that our young men and women will be ready to take their proper places in society. Today they learn. Tomorrow they lead." – Gregory Salton, Founder of the Salton Academy, 1954

PLAN
FOR
EXCELLENCE

CHAPTER
ONE

Jeff had no more doubts; someone was stealing food from the pantry. He ran over his checklist, his flashlight alternating between his mouth and his hand. Yesterday there had been fifteen cases of crackers. Today there was only fourteen. None of yesterday's meals had crackers in them. He would know. Ever since the Outbreak and the world had gone to hell, he had taken charge of the food supplies and taken on the role of cook.

He felt the tightness of fear in his chest, making it hard for him to breathe, making it feel like he was about to have an asthma attack. But he refused to let his mind go to that place again, to wonder what it had been like for *her*. No. No one would starve on his watch. Not now. Not ever again. He pushed the fear away with anger.

"'The Salton Academy prides itself on the well-rounded individual. Every student will know how to cook and clean as well as be educated to Salton's high standards.'" Jeff's voice rasped with sarcasm as he quoted from one of the school's many prep books. "Well, apparently, 'well-rounded' also means thievery."

As he added the case of missing crackers to his list of stolen food, Jeff decided it was time to talk to Principal Swenson about matters. At this rate the school would be out of food in the worst part of winter. There wouldn't be enough to feed the twenty-six people ensconced in the prep school turned safe haven in the apocalypse.

He closed the walk-in pantry door with a grimace. Why could no one ever look farther than next week? Didn't they understand the danger of tomorrow?

* * *

Shin Yoshida walked his normal patrol route since the Outbreak happened. First he walked the perimeter, peering through the lookout holes he had established in the academy's tall stone wall. He stopped and watched, looking for any sign of movement that might be trouble on its way. It was a lovely walk that ate away at the endless days and gave him something to do. He would still protect his charges. While on patrol he continued to wear his guard uniform. It was partly habit and partly functional. Though the primitive wash bucket cleaning in cold water was taking a toll on all of his clothing—uniforms included. Most of them sported carefully mended holes and repaired hems.

As Shin walked the perimeter closest to the campus proper, he looked inward and scanned the small academy, examining each building from the outside. Beyond the various garden sheds, there were seven main buildings. The four most important—the administration building, the Main Hall; the boys' dorm, Hadfield Hall; the girls' dorm, Bonny Hall; and the Commons—were set in a circle around the main quad. Set in the southwest of the campus, cattycorner between the Hadfield and Bonny Halls, was the non-denominational chapel. Privately, Shin believed the chapel was set there to remind the students that God was watching as they snuck into each others' rooms at night.

Set to the east, behind the Commons, was the Atherton Gymnasium for Excellence with its weight room, basketball court, and now defunct pool. It had been the highlight of entertainment during the quarter breaks. For three weeks at a time, four times a year, Shin had owned that building without fear of interrupting a student function. Set just south of the gym was the infirmary. Someone in their august wisdom had thought to put it next to the two places that caused the most injuries.

Once the perimeter patrol was done, each building would get its own patrol to make sure bored teenagers weren't destroying things for the hell of it. Shin varied the building order by whim. It kept the small set of students and faculty members on their collective toes. Secure though the Salton Academy was, no place in the world was 100% safe. Not since the Outbreak. This was his small way of reminding them of that.

Shin paused by the side of the Main Hall. He watched Professor Leeds exit the front door and head towards Bonny Hall. Shin did not like that man. Not at all. He glanced up at the third floor, seeking Sophia's room. He glimpsed movement but nothing more. Shin scowled and pondered the situation. He watched every single person on this campus. It was his job to protect them all. Even from themselves.

* * *

"Are you all right?"

Athena's question made his heart hurt as much as his body did. Forcing a smile, Evan nodded. "Yeah. Just tired. You know how it is."

She leaned back in his office chair. It wasn't standard issue for the Salton Academy but when your father ran the place you got special dispensation. In this case, Athena knew it was warranted. "Is it your medicine?"

Evan wouldn't look at her. He looked down at his hands, the fingers swelling with debilitating arthritis. He didn't like talking about his failings with his best friend and the one girl he could never have. "I'm getting by."

"How? It's been almost three months since…you know."

He knew. "I've been taking a half-dose for a while now. To make it last longer."

She tilted her head. "Is that actually working?" She gave him a critical once over, really looking at him, his swelling hands, and the stiff way he held his body.

"Well enough. Methotrexate takes a long time to ramp up but once it's in your system it's there for a while. It's helped with…everything." Evan continued look at his hands, the knuckles looking like they belonged in a man three times his age.

"You need to let your father know you're running out. It should be put on the list for the next supply run."

"It's a controlled substance. A medicine usually used for cancer patients. It's not like you can get it from the corner store these days. It always had to be ordered in advance."

Athena was quiet for a moment. "Still. It's about time we did a real pharmacy run. We're starting to get low on stuff."

Evan didn't answer that. The very idea of a supply run made his stomach hurt and his heart beat faster. The need to ask for a special request hurt even more.

* * *

4

Out of the window of her dorm room, Sophia saw Professor Leeds start to cross the quad from the main hall to the girls' dorm. Michael, he wanted her to call him when they were in private. She just couldn't do that. Ducking away from the window before he saw her Sophia thought about where she should hide today. She just didn't feel like being with him anymore. She hadn't figured out how to tell him and it was becoming a problem.

Sophia knew she would need to tell him and sooner rather than later. But, in the meantime, she would hide. It was easy enough to disappear in a building meant to house four hundred school girls and faculty. She would head up to her sanctuary in the attic. Work on making it even more secure in case of…the worst. At this point, she wasn't sure what the 'worst' would be but when it hit she planned to have a secured shelter in place for her and her friends.

* * *

Michael looked up to Sophia's dorm room. She wasn't sitting in the window but that was all right. She was usually where he wanted her. Usually. Lately she'd been busy with projects for that Harridan, Hood, who managed the girl's dorm. But today he had an itch that really needed to be scratched. He was starting to get bored with the girl but lovely young ladies were in short supply these days.

He slipped inside Bonny Hall. The quiet of the dorm building made him feel more like a thief in the night rather than the man of authority he was. Michael smiled, feeling all the more wicked and randy. He took the stairs up to the third floor two at a time, suppressing his urge to whistle. Mrs. Kimberly Hood did not approve of such things as whistling.

Room 313. He knocked then tried the door when there was no answer. It was locked. He frowned. Anger rising at being immediately thwarted. He pulled his school key ring from a pocket and used the Bonny Hall master key he wasn't supposed to have to unlock and open Sophia's door.

As one of the upperclassmen, Sophia had her own room. Decorated in tasteful green tartan, the room was neat and clean. Even the bed was made. Only the bright pink metal water bottle on the desk told him that a teenager girl lived in the room. Michael scowled at the empty room. Then he noticed the condensation on the water bottle showing that it was half full. He walked over and picked it up, smearing the wetness that clung its metal sides. The fresh chill of the water surprised him. This had been refilled from the bottled well water kept in one of the cold basement rooms and not all that long ago. He gulped down the cold water, finished it, and slammed the metal container back to the desk.

Sophia had been here. Now she wasn't. Michael scowled more as he closed and locked Sophia's door. She must have seen him coming. As he stalked the hallways of Bonny Hall, looking for the girl, he contemplated what her absence meant.

* * *

"As you see, sir, with the missing food and my projected consumption rate of the food left in the Commons we won't have enough to last the winter." Jeff pointed at the handmade graph. "In fact, we'll run out in the worst part of winter. We've got to do another supply run now…and put a lock on the pantry door."

Robert Swenson rubbed his face and looked at the earnest teenager. One of the youngest Eagle Scouts in the tri-cities area, Jeff was a miracle of preparation. Swenson simultaneously cursed and thanked Providence that the kid was one of the students had remained behind for the quarter break. He rarely saw the boy unless it was at meals or there was bad news.

"Any ideas on who is stealing the food?"

Jeff shook his head. "No. I'd have to start sleeping in there to know that. Or be in charge of *all* of the keys to the Commons."

Robert shook his head. Trusted or not, he couldn't allow a teenager to be the sole gatekeeper to the food. He looked at the list of stolen food again. Flats of canned goods and water. Cases of crackers, cereal, and cookies. All non-perishable food that could last a long time for one person. "I suppose you've got a list of what you believe we will need to survive the winter?"

"Yes, sir." Jeff couldn't keep the smile off his face. This was exactly what he wanted. The principal to depend on him. To see things his way. To *understand* the danger of an unplanned tomorrow. Jeff flipped the notebook page over and showed Robert the list. It included staples like rice, flour, and salt.

"No water?"

"No, sir. We've got that well pump in the Commons into the protect water table. It may have a mineral taste that we're not used to but it is safe and it's time we start using it. We have no idea when the running water will cease to run, or when it will become poisonous. One or both are likely and probably soon. I'll keep testing it but it's best to stick to the well for drinking water and the running water for everything else. Also, liquid is heavy. As it is, we're going to have to send four people on this run instead of three. The staples are needed. It's bland but it stretches a long way. And I can teach everyone how to cook bread over a fire. Fresh food will keep morale up. We can even make hard tack for the winter months. I know how."

The older man nodded. "All right. Set up a supply run draw." He sat back and looked at Jeff. He could tell the boy had more to say. "Anything else?"

"The dog—"

"No." Robert cut him off. "We've talked about this before. We're not going to do it again."

Jeff stood, taking his papers back. "It's a danger, sir."

"No. It's not. And we're not having this conversation again. Dismissed." Robert picked up the nearest folder and opened it. He looked down, not seeing the useless forms within as he waited for Jeff to leave.

"We *will* have to do something about it." Jeff's voice was soft as he walked to the principal's door. "Soon."

Once Jeff was gone, Robert sighed and muttered, "But not today." He knew Jeff was right about Evan's dog but he wasn't willing to do anything about it just yet. He had enough problems with his son. Killing the kid's dog wasn't going to be one of them.

* * *

Evan looked at the small round pills with despair and counted them again. Thirty. Just three doses. He counted out ten of the tiny two milligram pills, cupped them in his hand, and then dry swallowed the lot of them, relishing the bitter taste as the small pills stuck in his throat for a moment. That bitter taste meant a relief to the joint pain and swelling that came with his disease for the next week. At this point, the pills were boosting the medicine already in his system.

Twenty tiny pills.

He marked off the day on the calendar with a slash then gave it the small hash mark to remind him that he had taken one of his doses. With one week blending into another it was easy to forget whether or not he had taken a dose the week before or not. The rest of the pills he put back into the pill container he always kept on him and stuffed it in his pocket.

He sat there and thought about the pills in his pocket. He could cut them in half, taking half a dose weekly instead of all ten pills every other week. Evan wasn't sure which was more effective. Now that he told Athena about his need Nurse Krenshaw would know. He might as well talk to her to see what she thought.

It was nothing more than pure, dumb luck that he had received his medicine renewal in the mail the day before the Outbreak and everything went to hell. As soon as the Outbreak hit the news his father had locked down the Academy campus. No one in. No one out.

That didn't stop them from trying…and dying.

Now, he was dying by inches. He knew it. His father knew it. That's why, even though they both lived in Hadfield Hall, he hadn't seen is father for more than a week. Not even at meals in the Commons. His father had taken to eating meals in his office.

The rage and fear suddenly overwhelmed him once more and he swept everything on his desk onto the floor with a crash and clatter that no one would respond to. They never did. He looked at the mess for a moment, swiping at his tears with angry swollen fists that left red marks on his cheeks.

This wasn't living. This was barely surviving.

Then his Salton Academy training took over again. There were weekly room inspections for the freshmen, bi-monthly inspections for the sophomores, and then random monthly inspections for the upperclassmen. Demerits sucked and equated to lower classmen chores. Evan hunkered down over the mess of papers, books, pens, pencils, and other detritus from his desk. He picked up his Salton Academy mug. It was chipped. Good. Fuck this damn school.

His urge to throw the mug melted away as Joe, one of his few friends, appeared in his doorway. The two upperclassmen looked at each other but didn't say anything. Joe gave Evan an understanding nod then hunkered down next to his friend to help him pick up the mess. Evan nodded back with grateful half-smile.

* * *

Michael paced all four floors of Bonny Hall. No one. Where the hell was that girl? Or any of the girls for that matter? At this point, Michael wanted to take his frustration out on anyone he could find. His mind roamed from Sophia to the other girls he knew about. Melissa? No…besotted with Lee. Rose? A possibility but she seemed to be spending a lot of time with Shane. Toni? He smiled at the thought of his hands tangled in her dark hair. But no, he had seen Aaron and her making eyes at each other.

Seemed like the apocalypse, and the idea of a limited number of partners made the kids couple up faster than the idea of going to the Winter Formal alone. Michael frowned at that idea. Hell, the Harridan was looking good these days.

Then he remembered the water bottle in Sophia's room and the chill of the water. The basement. They had to be there. At least one of them. Kimberly had taken to giving the girls *fortifying* tasks to keep morale up. Michael picked up his pace and hoped that Sophia was in the basement. It was one place he hadn't had her yet. Too cold. But, the way he was feeling, a quickie would do.

Whistling as he came down the steps Michael wanted to make sure he was heard. If Sophia was down here, it would heighten her anticipation. If it was another girl, well, it wouldn't do to frighten her into thinking he wasn't human. These days, you couldn't be too sure.

"Hello?" Michael kept his voice light and listened.

"Hello. I'm in the root cellar."

The voice belonged to Rose. Michael nodded to himself. She

was pretty enough. A bit on the wild side outside of the Academy with dyed red hair and a tongue piercing. Perhaps it was time to feel her out. See if she'd be interested in a man instead of the boy she'd been hanging out with. He grinned at the idea of the tongue piercing and wondered what else she had pierced.

S wenson is fucking useless." Jeff scowled at his small group of
cohorts, Caleb, Steve, and Ron. "He doesn't seem concerned
at all that someone is stealing food or that we're going to run
out by mid-winter."

Steve shrugged. "Well, you're keeping him up-to-date."

"That's not enough. There are too many people here for too
little supplies. Not to mention that damn dog." Jeff shook his
head. Just thinking about the dog made him want to vomit. He
held onto that anger and the anger at the stolen food to keep
himself from panicking at the missing food, at the thought of
all of them slowly starving to death, at the knowledge that the
weak were fodder for the strong.

Caleb looked up from the comic he was leafing through.
"Gives me the creeps."

"It's a danger." Jeff warmed to his audience. This wasn't anything they hadn't already heard. He'd been complaining about the supply situation and the dog situation for a couple of weeks now. "Too many people's a danger. Not enough supplies is a danger. We're just lucky that the Outbreak happened between Summer and Fall Quarters. Otherwise more people would've stayed for the break." Jeff specifically didn't think about his friend, the one they had lost on the last supply run, and he certainly wouldn't think about *her*.

Ron, who hasn't said anything in weeks it seemed, raised his head and a finger. "So, there's a problem. A couple of them. What are we going to do about it? What can we do about it?" He gazed at Jeff with an expectant air.

Caleb and Steve shared an uneasy glance. They both knew about Ron's more violent tendencies, the ones he kept secret from the world. They also knew that if it came to a fight they wanted Ron on their side. Only Ron's long friendship with Jeff seemed to keep him in check. Without that, who knows what Ron would get into. In this case it really was the quiet one you needed to watch out for.

Jeff rubbed his goatee. He'd grown it since the Outbreak. It was one more means of protection. If infected blood splashed on his face, it would run down the outside of the goatee instead of into his mouth. Ever since he told the boys about it, and cut off his ponytail as handhold danger, the rest had followed suit with varying degrees of success. "What can we do about it?" He repeated the question, giving himself time to think.

Caleb and Steve sat up and watched Ron and Jeff with interest. Jeff wouldn't ever hear a bad word about Ron. The two had each other's backs. And, until this point, it had been nothing but complaints. Jeff would complain. They would listen. With Ron leading Jeff's train of thought perhaps they were going to finally do something and stop the missing food. Stop the worries about the dangers of an 'unplanned tomorrow.'

"I'm the cook. I can insist on the lock on the pantry door." Jeff's voice was distant with thought.

Ron nodded. "That will stop the stealing. Hopefully."

Jeff ran his fingers down the sides of his goatee. "The dog… it's a danger. We should kill it."

This time Ron smiled.

"But what about Swenson?" Caleb's voice cracked.

"Swenson be damned!" Jeff continued to watch Ron.

Ron continued to smile at Jeff and nodded. "We kill the dog. It's a danger. And what about the too many people thing?" His voice was soft, almost seductive.

"We kill them."

Now that he'd finally said what he'd been thinking about ever since he'd discovered the food thefts Jeff held his breath and waited. Caleb and Steve looked at each other, their eyes wide and disbelieving.

"We kill them." Ron repeated Jeff's words and tone then looked off to the side. "Kill how many of them?" He made the question sound academic.

Jeff frowned and thought about it. "There are twenty-six people on campus. If we get no more food at all we can only feed sixteen, seventeen, maybe. And that would be rationing it."

"We're not going to kill ten people." Caleb paused. "Are we?" He looked faintly sick to his stomach.

"No." Jeff shook his head. "Swenson's going to call for a supply run. Four people will be chosen."

"So we kill six?" Ron licked his lips and tilted his head, still not looking at anyone.

Steve and Caleb shared another uneasy glance.

"Maybe. Six is the upper limit. Especially if the supply run is successful." Jeff looked at his ever-present notebook. "If they aren't, we just don't let them back in. That takes care of four of them right off."

"Who and how?" Steve's voice was filled with both awe and revulsion. "How do we kill people without them trying to kill us back? How do we choose who should die?"

Jeff thought about it. "We wait to see who is going to go on the supply run. I'll make a list. We'll talk about it. And all agree."

"Make sure Melissa's name is on that supply run list." Ron's voice was far away.

"Why?" Caleb frowned. "How?"

"Because Lee will volunteer if Melissa goes."

Steve laughed. "You're just mad that she turned you down and Lee used to shove you in the broom closet."

Ron's look was venomous. "Does that matter?"

Jeff shook his head and cut off the squabbling before it began. "No. I'll make sure Melissa's on that list. And Evan. It's time Swenson realizes he's not really in charge here anymore. No matter what he thinks."

* * *

Athena sat across from Principal Swenson. "Thank you for seeing me, sir."

"My door is always open to Salton Academy students. I'm here for you." Robert smiled at her. It made him happy to see someone other than Jeff or his faculty coming to see him. "What can I do for you?"

"It's about Evan."

His smile faltered. This was not what he had expected. "What about him?"

"It's his medicine. He's running out." Athena worked to keep the fear and concern out of her face. Instead, she strove to look and sound like the expertly trained nurse she would never be.

Robert sat back and looked around the walls of his well-appointed office. His degrees and certificates adorned the walls in proud display and many of the awards the Salton Academy had won sat is prefect place with shiny splendor. For all his success there was one failure wedded to his name that he could do nothing about. It was the hardest failure of all. "How long?"

"He told me that he has about a month of the methotrexate left which means he probably only has a couple of weeks. He's suffering."

Bowing his head, the man thought for a long moment about the son he no longer knew. Then he nodded to himself and looked at Athena. "There will be a supply run soon. I'll have them go to the hospital to pick up the medicine. You should give me a list of needed supplies for the infirmary."

Relief made her pale face light up. "Okay. Good. I will. I've been keeping track. I can write you a list now. Nurse Krenshaw and I talked about what we needed this week."

Robert nodded and gestured to pen and paper on his desk. He watched her write, wondering about her and wondering about Evan. "Is there anyone else with illnesses that I need to be concerned about?"

Athena didn't look up as she wrote. "Jeff has asthma but it's under control. He doesn't even take an inhaler for it. But we have do have a few rescue inhalers. Toni has allergies but there's not much we can do about that."

"Except add allergy medicine to the medical needs list."

She nodded, wrote that down, and paused, thinking. "Everyone else is relatively healthy. I suppose we could all use Vitamin D for the winter season. Evan is really our main concern."

He noted the studied casualness of the last statement. It seemed that she had been spending a lot of time with his son. And without her family's privilege and prejudice to get in the way. "How is he? Really?"

"Doing as well as someone with a crippling autoimmune disorder with limited medicine can be. He hurts." She glanced up at him. "When's the last time you talked to him?"

"Recently." Robert lied without blinking. "But, as his father, he doesn't tell me much."

She nodded and opened her mouth to say he should try harder, thought better of it, and shook her head with a smile. "This is all I can think of."

Robert took the offered piece of paper. "I'll add it to the list. Thank you. Dismissed." He continued to look at the paper, his eyes rolling over the wish list, taking them in with little interest. Instead he listened to her leave and close the door behind her.

* * *

"What are you doing back here?" Michael tilted his head and looked into the darkened root cellar, lit with a battery power camp lantern. The room had a dirt floor with a stone walkway on one side. It smelled of must and vegetables.

Rose raised the lantern to show off the room's shelves, containing rows and rows of green tomatoes. "Checking to see if any of these had ripened or rotted. We had to bring in the last of the tomatoes as the weather turned chill. Now, we wait to see which will make it and which won't."

"You've got a deft hand at that." Michael moved into the doorway, acting as if he was trying to get a better look. Mostly, he was trying to catch the girl's scent. Baby powder with a hint of acrid sweat. Not bad at all. The electricity was gone but water still flowed. It made for damn cold showers but kept those still rattling around the school fairly clean.

She shrugged. "I like tomatoes. As Mrs. Hood says, 'If the individual works to their passions and strengths, the community as a whole prospers.'"

Michael raised an eyebrow. "Does she now?"

Rose nodded. "I'm good at gardening. We can't do much of it right now but when the spring comes the hot house will be my domain."

"Thinking that far ahead, are we?" Michael lowered his voice. "I guess I'm a little more concerned with immediate…needs."

She looked up at the sudden purr in the teacher's voice and didn't like the way he was looking at her. "Oh? Um…"

Michael nodded. "Like safety and security. And comfort." He smiled and leaned down toward her. "Is there anything you need? Anything at all?"

Rose took a step back and could not believe this *professor* was suddenly hitting on her. No, he couldn't be doing that. He wouldn't. He was a *professor*. Even if it was the apocalypse. "Uh. No." She shook her head.

"You sure?" Michael licked his lips in a deliberate and sensuous motion. He wanted to laugh at how big her eyes got. As skittish as a doe, she would be fun to chase.

"Professor Leeds!" The strident voice carried well down the echoing hall. "I trust you have a very good reason for interrupting my student in her duty?"

Michael grimaced and almost winced with every clack of the Harridan's sensible heels. He put a smile in his voice as he turned to the dorm mistress approaching the root cellar door at a rapid pace. "Yes, Kimberly. I came to see if you ladies needed anything. I was just talking to Rose about her ripening tomatoes."

From her matching pant suit to her curly black hair in a bun to her ebon skin scrubbed clean with icy cold water, Kimberly Hood was all business. "I prefer you call me Mrs. Hood, Professor Leeds. The end of civilization as we know it is no reason to forget your manners." She put her hands on her generous hips.

"Yes, Mrs. Hood." Michael heaved a sigh. "I thought we'd gotten past all that."

Kimberly stared at him for a long moment. "Well?"

"Well what?"

She looked between Rose and Michael. "Did she tell you that we'd like to have another honey pot moved to the basement?"

Rose shook her head. "I forgot, Mrs. Hood. And speaking of which…I gotta…" She stopped at the look in the dorm mistress' eyes. "May I be excused?"

Kimberly nodded with approval. "You may. I will see you in a bit to discuss your progress."

Rose ducked her head and hurried by Michael, refusing to look at him. Kimberly noticed how Michael watched the girl's quick retreat and narrowed her eyes. "So, you'll get some boys and get it done?"

Michael looked at Kimberly. "Huh?"

"The honey pot. We want it moved into the same room as the first."

"Oh, right. Yes. I'll get it done." He sighed inwardly. The honey pot idea was a good one. Not that they actually used them right now. But it seemed that the Harridan was taking no chances with the coming of winter. They were all lucky that the school had started breaking ground on astronomy tower in the west end of the academy land.

"Thank you." She took his elbow. "I'll see you out. Let me know when you need to get in the basement loading ramp."

* * *

"Nurse Krenshaw didn't really know what the best way to stretch my medicine was. She told me to try the half dose thing so I had a consistent level of health and pain. Neither good nor bad. Just uncomfortable all the way around."

Evan sat with his back against the cold tile and watch Beauregard as he shuffled and moaned a low keening sound. He hunched his shoulders and pretended that it was a soft howl. He had had the dog since he was a puppy and it was the one thing in this damn place that was all his. It was the one thing in this damn life that had loved him without reservation. Beau had saved him from the one zombie that had gotten through the school's defenses. And this was his reward.

The black lab suddenly snarled and threw himself at the equipment cage, trying to get to the teen. Evan winced as the dog tore part of his muzzle away, revealing gleaming teeth in rotting gums. If he had realized that Beau would hurt himself trying to get to him he would've connected the harness chain to the back of the cage instead of the side. Along with the bite mark on his shoulder the dog was missing flesh on parts of his paws, his legs, and now his muzzle. His once glossy black eyes were cloudy as if the dog was suffering from cataracts.

"Sometimes I think you got the better end of the deal." Evan's voice was soft and filled with longing. "No pain. No realization of death. No cares except to feed."

He shifted into another, less pain-filled position. "I never liked this school. I didn't like it when dad divorced mom. I didn't like it when he got custody. I really didn't like it when he gave me a dorm room. I suppose I should've been happy. I had my own room with almost no rules. Except to do well." Evan mimicked his father's voice with a sneer. "'You're a Salton Academy boy now, son. Be proud. Make me proud. As one of my students I'm going to expect excellence from you.'"

He scoffed at the dog. "But nothing more than that. The only reason he got custody, that he wanted custody, was because it hurt mom." He heaved a sigh and struggle to numbed feet as Beau scrabbled claws at the underside of the cage door with a futile fury. "Never thought this place would become a prison for both of us."

Turning, Evan picked up the lantern and limped from the room. "Yeah, you got the better end of the deal." He closed the door to the gym office with a soft thump.

CHAPTER
THREE

Robert Swenson looked over the assembled students and faculty of the Salton Academy. *This is what's left of civilization,* he thought with regret. *This once proud school is reduced to this: twenty-one students and five faculty.* He clenched his jaw. This was the one thing he was a complete success at. He would not allow it to fall into disrepair. Jeff was correct. He needed to take a firm hand here.

"Ladies and gentlemen, it has come to my attention that someone has been stealing…taking…food from the Commons pantry. Flats of canned goods and other such consumables have been taken without permission." He ignored Jeff's offered list. "If these things are returned, no punishment will be given. It was not explicitly stated that we were rationing food. It is being explicitly stated now. As such, the Commons pantry will be locked and a few notable people will have the key. Myself, Mrs. Hood, and Jeff."

Robert looked around at the faces of his people and saw a range of emotion from confusion to anger to apathy. He opened his mouth to speak when the engineering teacher, Professor Leeds, interrupted him.

"If the Commons pantry is locked how can anyone return what they've taken?"

The principal gave him a sharp look. "Is that a confession?"

"No, Principal Swenson. Just an observation." Michael grinned at him. "Just pointing out the obvious."

Jeff took a step forward. "The stolen…missing…supplies can either be left outside the pantry door or may be given to me directly. I'm the one putting the meal plans together and executing them." He glanced at the principal, who nodded. "I promise anonymity to anyone who brings the supplies directly to me." He took a step back and picked up a black bag.

Robert gave him a look and Jeff returned the gaze as if waiting for orders. He would have to talk to the boy about making such declarations without talking to him first. Then again, Jeff was a take charge kind of kid. He turned back to the assembled people. "Professor Leeds, does that satisfy you?"

Michael's grin widened. "Yes, that's one thing that satisfies me."

Ignoring that thought, Robert continued with his announcements. "As there's missing supplies and, as we will be shortly moving from fall into winter, it's time for another supply run." He paused at the sudden unease and stirring before him. "I understand this is a frightening thing but it is necessary for Salton Academy to survive the coming snows. We've only had one run since the Outbreak and if we didn't have to do this we wouldn't."

Jeff took a step forward again as the room continued to buzz. He raised his voice to be heard. "As agreed upon the last time we had a supply run, those going are drawn from the bag. Once a person has gone once they do not need to go again until everyone in the Academy has gone. All names are in the bag without exception. Four people need to go this time."

The room hushed into complete silence as Jeff dipped his hand into the black bag. He didn't have to fear. He went last time. It was an awful experience he didn't want to do again anytime soon. Again, he refused to let his mind dwell on what happened when he was 'out there' last. He had better things to do now. Shaking his hand, the piece of paper Jeff had tucked into his sleeve fell into his cupped palm. Pulling the folded paper out he handed it to the principal without looking at it. He didn't need to. He knew whose name was on it.

"Melissa Branson," Swenson read and looked up. The pale girl with shaggy brown hair flushed and clutched the boy next to her.

The boy immediately stood. "I volunteer as tribute." His voice was laconic and unconcerned.

Jeff blinked in false surprise and shook his head. "You went with me last time. Your name isn't in the bag."

"Don't care. If Melissa's going, I'm going."

Jeff exchanged a look with Swenson and shrugged. Swenson nodded. "All right. Along with Melissa, Lee Harton will go on the supply run." He gave Jeff a gesture for another name and took the offered folded paper. "Nicholas Alexander."

The slim black boy shook his head at his luck, muttering under his breath. Then he nodded at the principal. Not only was he a senior—if such things still counted—he was, had been, Leeds' teaching assistant. Michael clapped the boy on the shoulder in sympathy.

Jeff handed the last folded slip to Swenson and the crowd grew that much quieter. He opened and read. "Evan—" He stopped, looking horrified. His eyes darted to his son and then back at Jeff who continued to look straight ahead. Swenson's lipped compressed into a thin white line of anger for a moment. Then he read the full name. "Evan Swenson."

Evan patted Athena's hand and stood, even as she shook her head, mouthing her denial. Then Joe stood. "I'll go in Evan's place. We want this supply run to succeed." He spoke in a matter-of-fact tone. No accusation. No malice. No joy.

"Joe, you don't…" Evan shook his head.

"You're in no shape. If Lee can volunteer, so can I." Joe nodded to the others going. "We'll be fine."

Everyone turned to Swenson for his final word. Robert nodded. "Quite right. Volunteers are allowed."

"Okay." Jeff broke through the babble. "Mel, Lee, Nicholas, Joe, see me tomorrow. We'll get you outfitted and give you the list. You'll be going for staples and for medical supplies."

The students and the faculty stood and clumped into gossiping groups, ignoring Principal Swenson as he watched the crowd. "That's all for now. Everyone is dismissed." Only one person looked at him: Evan. For a moment they stared at each other. Then Evan turned in a deliberate gesture to talk to Athena.

I am losing control, Robert thought, fear growing into a cold lump in his stomach. Jeff gave him a tight smile and a nod before walking away. Robert watched him go to his group of friends, knowing that he was going to have to do something about the boy. He wasn't sure what. He had not expected this level of betrayal from the student who had appeared most loyal to him.

* * *

Michael grabbed Sophia's arm at the elbow before she could escape. He leaned to her with a smile, his body hiding his hard grip. "I missed you earlier today. Where were you?"

Startled, Sophia tried to pull her arm away from him and whimpered deep in her throat as his hand tightened, bruising her. "I-I was working. Mrs. Hood. A project."

He knew it for the lie it was and his smile widened a little, baring his teeth. Her eyes widened and she looked away, knowing he saw the lie. "A project. What project?"

Looking for anyone who could save her, the assembled people were leaving. There was no one and Sophia realized she had to do something now. She raised her eyes and took a breath. "Yes, Professor Leeds, a project for Mrs. Hood. In the attic. I'm sure you have the boys fixing and fortifying Hadfield Hall. Don't you?" She spoke louder than she needed to, drawing eyes to them.

Snatching his hand away from her Michael took on a more formal posture. He tilted his head and nodded. "A project then." His voice was thoughtful as he contemplated her defiance. "We'll have to talk more about this…later." It was a promise.

Sophia turned away with a flounce of hair and a spring in her step. She held her head high as she walked over to the knot of Bonny Hall girls clustered about Melissa. Kimberly watched her come and caught her eyes. Sophia saw the question and concern. She shook her head and Kimberly looked away. Sophia rubbed her sore arm and wondered once more if she shouldn't just confess everything to the dorm mistress and get help.

Michael watched Sophia and avoided the Harridan's accusing eyes. Smirking to himself he wondered if he'd have to teach the girl a lesson and remind her that he wasn't a student she could just throw away when she was done with him. It might be a fun lesson to give.

"Will there be anything else, Professor?" The diffident voice of Shin Yoshida, came from behind him.

Michael shook his head, surprised. He hadn't realized the small man was there and wondered how much the security guard had overheard. Giving Shin a careful look, he saw no accusation on the older man's smooth face. "No." He gestured to the push broom in Shin's hand. "Keeping busy?"

Shin nodded. "There's only so much patrolling we can do. The walls keep the monsters out. I prefer where I live to remain clean. So, I clean."

"Makes sense. Don't suppose you do requests…like my suite? Bring in firewood for the fireplace?" The joke fell flat as Shin did not respond and Michael cleared his throat. "Well, better get back before it gets too late."

"Have a good evening, Professor." Shin watched Michael leave and wondered if he needed to clean up that mess. His job of protecting the students did not end with the Outbreak or the zombies.

* * *

Robert paused a long time before he knocked on Lee's door. He listened as the door was unlocked and smiled at Lee's surprise. "May I come in?"

"Yes, sir." Lee stepped back, letting the principal enter.

Robert looked around. The room was as neat and orderly as if it were to be inspected tomorrow. The upperclassman's desk was covered in maps. Some of the spots inside and outside the tri-cities area were circled. Most of the places within were circled and crossed off. He turned and looked at Lee who waited patiently for him to speak.

Robert paused, not knowing how to start, then plunged on. "You didn't have to volunteer. It was brave of you."

"I did. Melissa means the world to me and I will do what I must to protect her."

Even if that means going into infested territory with her, Swenson marveled. He contemplated the tall and handsome young man. A favorite at the school he would have gone so far if the world had not gone to hell. Built like a marine, Lee had managed to keep the look despite the lack of power. He suspected Melissa cut his hair for him.

"Sir, what do you need?"

"Ever one to cut through the bullshit." Robert ignored the raised eyebrow. "I have a special request of you. Not for me. For Evan." He paused, then continued on as Lee listened patiently. "It's his medicine. The methotrexate. He's running out. If he doesn't get more he's going to die." Robert looked away. "My son will die a long, painful, lingering death and there's nothing I can do about it."

Lee shifted papers on his desk until he came up with a list. "If it's available, where will we find it?" He added the methotrexate to the list of special requests he'd been keeping.

Robert bowed his head. Part of him wanted to weep. Part of him wanted to hug Lee. Instead, he said, "You can check the pharmacies. It has to be prescribed. But, because it's a cancer medicine, you'll probably have to check any hospitals you come across."

Lee nodded. "Let's hope it doesn't come to that."

The tone in Lee's voice made Robert look up. Then he remembered Lee had gone on the last run. Both he and Jeff had come back a little different. Niall hadn't come back at all. "That bad?" He imagined the amount of the dead and undead in and around hospitals.

"That bad." Lee straightened, putting his pen down. "And other requests?"

Being a hero is for the young, Robert thought and shook his head. "No. Thank you."

CHAPTER
FOUR

Jeff checked over the four students, adjusting things as they went. All of them had heavy jackets, backpacks, and weapons. "You know the drill, Lee. I recommend you be in charge. Stay away from hospitals and churches. That's where people gathered and died." He handed Lee one of the radios. "We'll do a radio check twenty minutes after you leave the gates. And there will be someone manning this radio 24/7 to let you guys back in when you have the supplies."

He moved to Melissa and adjusted the jacket, not looking her in the face. "Try to stick to the blunt weapons as much as possible. Noise draws them. Don't use the guns unless you really have to and your ammo is limited." He glanced up at her and was disappointed to see her looking at Lee.

Jeff moved to Nicholas. "Lee and Nicholas have copies of

the list of things we need. They're broken out in tiers. Tier one is the list of must-haves. We need these to survive as a community. Tier two are the nice-to-haves and tier three are the special requests from individuals."

Nicholas shifted and readjusted himself after Jeff was done with him. "What do we do about survivors?"

Joe answered before Jeff could. "We bring them back, of course." He brushed Jeff's hands off him. "I got it, dude. Like Lee, this ain't my first rodeo. May not be an Eagle Scout but I got training."

Jeff frowned at the rebuke and stepped back. "If you lose the radio we'll have look-outs between 10 and 2. Use the flare gun. We'll know to come and let you guys back in the gates. We're not going to expect you for at least three days but look-outs will start tomorrow."

Principal Swenson stepped up. "Be careful. We need those supplies but we want you guys back safe and sound. For all I know, we're the last civilization in the tri-cities."

Lee offered his hand to Robert. "We got this. We'll see you soon."

Then there was nothing more to say. Shin lead the teenagers to one of the small side doors in the stone barrier designed to make ground work just outside the walls easier to maintain. It was now the only easy way in and out of the Salton Academy property. The main gate was blocked by a large truck and the back gate was blocked by several cars pressed up to the bars. The eight foot stone wall, topped with spiked iron adornments, made for a formidable barrier for the slow moving but unrelenting zombies.

"I'll be here every afternoon on this side of the door. You know "Shave and a Haircut"?" Shin gazed at Lee with calm eyes.

"Yeah." He tapped out the rhythm.

Shin tapped back his part, two bits. "That's the call and response. All of you, memorize it. I'll let you in whether or not I've been given permission." His voice was low enough that only the four of them could hear what he said.

The four teenagers looked at each other and nodded. The serious look on Shin's face made his words that much more ominous. As one, they realized just how dangerous everything was inside, as well as outside, the protective walls of the Salton Academy grounds.

Lee took a breath. "Okay. Let's go."

Shin looked through the three peepholes before until he was satisfied that no zombies lurked immediately beyond the gate. Then he let the teenagers through.

*　*　*

Kimberly Hood looked at the assembled girls and only other female adult on campus. They all crowded into her sitting room. Rose and Toni sat together on the couch while Pria and Maya stood and leaned against the wall, their shoulders touching in sisterly companionship. Sophia and Athena sat at Nancy Krenshaw's feet, the only trained medical person they had. Julie sat on the arm of Nancy's chair. Kimberly stood before them all.

"I am beginning to believe we have a problem with Professor Leeds." Kimberly glanced at Rose. "I've found him in the hall several times when he shouldn't be. Yesterday, I found him menacing Rose."

"I don't know for sure but I think he was flirting with me." Rose's voice was soft and embarrassed.

"Have any of you had any uncomfortable meetings with Professor Leeds in the last couple of months? Since the lockdown?" Kimberly looked at her girls.

"He's flirted me with me. Or used to. I ignored it. I'm with Aaron. But…I've caught him watching me," Toni admitted. "But he hasn't done anything more than that. Just watched me. It's been weird."

Nancy's voice quavered a little. "I'm too old for that sort of thing. He likes his girls young." She looked at Kimberly. "And I've had to treat more than one girl worried about pregnancy after having been with him. I always reported these up the chain but nothing's come of it."

Kimberly fought back her anger. "Rape?" The girls winced at the blunt and ugly word.

"No. The man can be very charming."

Sophia looked at her hands, debating if she should admit to being with Michael. The thought of it made her flush hard and her stomach dropped away.

"But the principal let this pass?"

Nancy nodded. "The Leeds family was very, very rich and always donated to the Academy."

"But…with a student?"

It was the horror in Mrs. Hood's voice that moved Sophia to speak. She decided that she'd rather face the dorm mistress' anger and punishment than Michael's now unwanted advances. "I…I have been with him." The room stilled and Sophia looked at her hands. "He *can* be charming. But he's not anymore. I don't want to be with him anymore and he's not getting the hint." She risked a glance up at Mrs. Hood.

Her face was unreadable. No condemnation or encouragement in it. "Have you told him no directly?"

Sophia shook her head. "Just been avoiding him. But I couldn't avoid him last night. He was mad." She slid her sleeve up and showed everyone the bruise Michael left on her arm just above the elbow.

Nancy shifted to look at the bruise and shook her head. "Nothing I can do for that."

Kimberly caught Sophia's eyes. "I won't say I'm not disappointed but this is not your fault. *You* are sixteen. *He* is a grown man and should never have pursued you." She paused. "He *did* pursue you?"

Sophia nodded. "He was…charming. He made me feel better about…things."

"Yes. The last three months have been difficult. I understand. However…" She pointed at the girl. "The next time you see him you need to be upfront and tell him no. Tell him in no uncertain terms that you are no longer interested. Then we'll see what he does." Kimberly scowled, worry lines creasing her forehead. "In the meantime, I'll have a few words with Principal Swenson about matters. And the rest of you, ladies, buddy system from now on. Sooner or later someone is going to decide the rules don't apply to them."

"Mrs. Hood?" Sophia's voice held a note of fear. "He has a key to my room."

"What?" The black woman shifted, her scowl deepening. "You should've known better!"

Sophia shook her head, her blond hair flying. "I didn't give him my extra copy. I don't know how he got it."

"How do you know he has a key to your room?"

"Yesterday I saw him coming and hid. I left a bottle of water on my desk. When I came back, the bottle was empty and one of my figurines was knocked over. It was him. I know it was. He wanted me to know he could get into my room anytime he wanted."

Kimberly and Nancy exchanged troubled glances. "Put a chair under your doorknob when you go to sleep until I tell you otherwise." The dorm mistress met the uncomfortable gazes of each of the other girls. "That goes for all of you, whether or not you have a roommate. Just to be sure. If we have even one more incident like that we're going to shift into a common sleeping room for safety and the conservation of heat. I don't want to have to do that until it gets too cold for privacy but I will do what I need to do to protect you all."

The chorus of "Yes, ma'am" and "Yes, Mrs. Hood" was subdued and reluctant. Kimberly knew they didn't want to think about the worst happening but, at this point, they had no other choice. Michael Leeds' actions had proven he could not be trusted. She exchanged another significant glance with the nurse and wondered what they could do about the situation.

* * *

Jeff waited until he saw Shin close and lock the side door to start his twenty minute timer. He sat under a tree, out of sight, holding the radio at hand with an earbud in, listening for noise. He wanted privacy for what was to come. From his advantage point he could see both Hadfield and Bonny Halls. Shin entered the former as Mrs. Hood and Nurse Krenshaw exited. The two women had their heads together and he couldn't hear what they were saying. He lost interest when they entered Bonny Hall and disappeared from sight.

His palms were sweating with the anticipation of what was coming. He wondered if they were going to turn around and charge right back when he gave them his ultimatum. Privately, he wished Lee had not gone on the supply run. He liked the guy. But he had to keep Ron happy. That way Ron would back him in the next part of the plan.

Finally, twenty minutes was up and the radio crackled to life in his ear. Jeff grinned. "Showtime." He pressed the button to talk. "I hear you. Over. Change of plans, Lee. You got that list I gave you? Over. Yeah. You guys need to get every single item in tier one or we're not going to let you back in. Over. Not kidding. Someone's been stealing food and if we don't get everything on that list we won't survive the winter. That's the price for you guys to get back in. Over."

Jeff winced a little at the response and bared his teeth all the more. "Good luck with that. Over and out." He pulled the earbud from his ear before he heard Lee's response and turned off the radio. He was shaking and sweating but he felt great. Eventually, Lee and the rest would come to understand that this was all for the good of the academy and that Jeff's extra motivation had been the right thing. No matter what he sat to the guys he wouldn't lock the supply team out. That just wasn't right.

He got up and headed back to the dorms, stopping halfway to watch Mrs. Hood come storming out of Bonny Hall like a woman going to war. He waited until she had disappeared around the corner, headed towards the main hall where Swenson's office was. Jeff shook his head. He wasn't sure who had done what but he was glad he wasn't on the receiving end of Mrs. Hood's ire.

* * *

"You *knew* about this?" Kimberly's voice took on a dangerous tone and she clenched her fists.

Robert held up both of his hands in a futile calming gesture. "Not about Leeds and Sophia. No. I knew he had a preference for young women but he's never forced them. In fact, half the time, they've pursued him. He's only human after all."

"I don't believe this. This is exactly why I refused to move

the girls to Hadfield Hall. Too much opportunity for abuse."
Kimberly paced back and forth. "You do realize what Leeds is
doing is called statutory rape, don't you?" She looked at his face.
He would not let meet her eyes. "And you let it go on here? You
let him keep his job?"

"Now, Kimberly, I did bring it up to the board. Not one of
those girls, or their parents, wanted to pursue that avenue. The
board decided it best not to bring that sort of scandal on the
Salton Academy." He kept his voice at its most reasonable best
despite the headache the clacking her shoes were giving him.

"It's rape and it's illegal!"

"The board did reprimand him."

"Reprimand him how? A note in his file?" Her fury morphed
into disbelief as Swenson looked away from her. That must have
been exactly what happened. "You've got to be kidding me. And
you let it happen on your watch. You disgust me." Her voice was
low and filled with venom.

Robert stood, his voice rising with his anger. "Not one of
those girls were hurt. Not one was even withdrawn from the
academy. No one was hurt. It's a victimless crime!"

Kimberly turned and looked at him. "He left bruises on
Sophia's arm. He's got a master key to Bonny Hall. What's it
going to take, Robert? A bruised and bleeding girl on the floor?
Or a dead one?"

He collapsed back into his chair and stared at his desk.
"What do you want me to do? It's not like I can banish him
from the campus."

"Why not?"

Robert looked up, startled. "It would be unconscionable. He
would die out there."

"So, you'd rather have him in here, with us, abusing the girls?" When Robert didn't respond Kimberly leaned on the desk. "If you won't do something about this, I will." She turned and strode from the office without waiting for a response.

"Be my guest," he muttered and shook his head. Robert uselessly shuffled the papers around on his desk, fighting the despair that threatened to overwhelm him. First Jeff's betrayal. Now this. He glanced at Evan's picture and sighed. The smiling teenager was a stranger to him.

Robert knew really should go visit his son and see how he's doing. "I should tell him I've sent Lee for his medicine." Instead of getting up and seeking out his son the principal of the Salton Academy turned his back on the picture and stared out the window at the empty campus quad and its untidy lawn.

* * *

"Didn't expect Joe to volunteer for Evan." Jeff leaned back in his chair. He looked at Ron. "But you were right. If Melissa went, Lee went." He fiddled with his Swiss Army knife, pulling open each of the tools one by one until it was completely open. Then he closed them all. It was a Swiss Army Eagle Scout Explorer with everything from scissors to a magnifying glass to a reamer with a sewing eye to numerous blades and other useful tools. His sister had given him the knife on his fourteenth birthday. His heart sped up at the thought of his dead sibling and he turned his thoughts back to the conversation.

"Joe has a crush on Evan. He's bi, you know. At least, that's what I've heard."

"Really?" Jeff looked thoughtful. "Didn't know that. I know Caleb and Steve are, you know…"

"Fucking?" Ron shrugged. "Whatever. It keeps Steve from

pining after me. I just don't swing that way. Or any way for that matter. Better things on my mind."

Jeff knew better than to point out that Ron had had a serious thing for Melissa and they all knew it. Then again, in all the years he'd known Ron, Melissa was the only person to attract him. No wonder he took her rejection so hard. "Steve's been in love with you for ages. I think Caleb's just a diversion until he can convince you to take a walk on the sausage side." Jeff laughed, fiddling with the magnifying glass, staring at the edges of a hole in his pants. He would have to fix that soon.

Ron, lying on Jeff's bed, turned over and gazed at him. "So, what was that look Swenson gave you when he saw Evan's name? It was like you kicked his puppy."

"I kinda did. Back when we all made the agreement that everyone went on supply runs and no one had to go twice until everyone had gone once. Including staff."

"And?"

"Swenson asked me to keep Evan's name out of the bag. He didn't care about his own name but his precious boy needed to be protected." He put his Swiss Army knife back in a pocket and picked up a pen, clicking it open and closed several times. "In exchange, I got to run the Commons."

"What made you change your mind?"

Jeff scowled. "That fucking dog. We're never going to be secure while that thing is inside the walls. Swenson won't do anything about it because it's Evan's dog."

Ron sat up. "So, we're gonna kill it?"

"Yes." Jeff clicked the pen a couple more times. "It's why I wanted Evan gone on the supply run. So we could kill the thing in peace. We've let it endanger us for too long."

"How we gonna do it?" Ron licked his lips.

"Shoot it. The sound should be muffled inside the gym with those sound dampening walls. And even if it's not, no one is going to blame us for killing one zombie dog."

* * *

Evan, who had come looking for company, stood outside Jeff's door, listening to the boys he thought were his friends, talk about killing the one thing he loved above all else. He slipped away before they could discover him. Fury clouded his mind as he went. To think he was coming to thank Jeff for thinking of the academy, for keeping such good track of the supplies, and for making sure they were all safe.

* * *

"I get to be there, right?"

Jeff nodded. "Yeah but I think we're going to have to deal with Swenson first."

Ron grinned and rubbed his hands together. "He's on the list, eh?"

"Top of the list but we're going to have to make it look like an accident."

"Or a suicide."

"Or a suicide." Jeff looked thoughtful. "Yeah. And I think I've got just the place for it."

Pria and Maya stood side by side in the fourth floor suite they had taken over and had quietly fortified into a bunker. Before them, in the back bedroom closet, was all of the stolen food. It was enough to keep two people alive for many weeks. Months if they were careful. They contemplated the stash for a long time.

"Do you think we should return it?" Maya toyed with the keys in her hand, the only keys she knew of for this particular suite.

Ever practical, Pria shook her head. "No. We can't do it anonymously and I don't trust Jeff. There's something off about him."

"You think he'd turn us in?"

"I don't know. But the last thing father told me was to make sure you were safe. This is the only thing I can think of. If things get crazy we can hide up here, lock the door, and keep really quiet until things stop being crazy."

Maya gave her sister a half hug. "I know it's hard. Because we don't look like them, we don't worship like them, they would abandon us first."

Pria nodded. "Yes. So we keep our secrets."

"Okay. What about Professor Leeds?"

She gave a small scoff. "He doesn't like dark meat. He can't look at Mrs. Hood without a sneer. I think we're safe enough."

Maya looked at her arm and coffee colored skin. "I don't know. I think he might do so down the line. We may be last choice but we're still girls."

Pria pulled a knife from her pocket. "He won't touch us. I swore to father I'd protect you and I meant it."

Smiling her gratitude Maya led Pria from the fourth floor suite, closing and locking the doors behind them. If nothing else, they always had this sanctuary.

* * *

This time when Michael went looking for Sophia she was exactly where he expected her to be. She sat in the bell tower of the main hall, bundled up against the cold. The weather wasn't bad but there was a bite in the air that promised the forthcoming winter was going to be a cold one. He saw no surprise on her face as he closed the door and walked over to the two lookout chairs.

"Hello, darlin'." He gave her his most charming smile.

"Professor Leeds." Sophia turned back to scanning the field beyond the side gate.

"I thought we were beyond such formalities." He reached down to touch her hair and frowned as she pulled away. "You're mad at me. Why?"

Sophia got up and walked away from him. "I just don't want to be touched."

So, he thought, *it was going to be a chase.* Maybe she was testing him. Maybe she felt he had taken her for granted and he needed to prove his desire. Michael moved to stand close behind her. "You know I love you." He wrapped his arms around her.

Sophia stiffened. "Stop." She squirmed and twisted.

He let her go just enough so he could see her face. "Why? You like it when I touch you."

"Not anymore."

That hurt more than expected. He let her go but didn't move away. She would not look at him. "Why not? What did I do wrong?"

Now she looked at him. "Nothing. Everything. I don't know. I just don't want to be with you anymore."

"I never hurt you. We had some good times, didn't we?" He leaned towards her. "Didn't we?"

"We did. But now..." She shook her head. "I just don't want...to anymore."

Michael took a step back. She had begun to say, 'I don't want you.' "It's the Harridan. She told you to break it off with me. Damn bitch."

"No!" Sophia rounded on him, her hands shaking and her knees threatening to buckle. "When we got together I was scared. My whole family was gone. You comforted me, promised to protect me. But now..." She stopped, her eyes saying what her mouth was not willing to say yet. *I don't need you.*

The fury rose but he put a clamp on it. It was Hood. It had to be her. Silently he swore he'd deal with the meddlesome woman. "I see. And now that everything seems safe and secure, I'm just not worth it anymore."

"It's not you. It's me. I've changed. I'm the one who...I just don't want *anyone* right now." It was a lie, of course. She did have her eye on another boy. Sweet, soft-spoken Ken. But she couldn't say that to Professor Leeds. Sophia raised a hand then dropped it. "Please, Professor Leeds, I'm sure there's someone else."

Michael couldn't stand the pity in her voice. He let some of the fury go. "Oh, yeah. And where the hell is this someone else supposed to be? Hmm? I love you, Sophia, and this is what I get. Thanks for nothing." He started to stalk away, then stopped with his hand on the door. "This isn't over. Not yet. Not until I say so. You just think about that and think about how you're going to apologize for hurting me. You got it?" When she didn't respond he let his voice rise. "You got it? Answer me."

Pale and shaken, Sophia nodded, "I-I got it."

"Good. I'll be in my suite. You'd better come soon, before my patience wears out."

* * *

Jeff flourished a piece of paper at his friends. "It's done. I've got the list."

"Which list?" Steve looked up from his crossword puzzle.

"The List," Ron said, sitting straighter, his eyes gleaming. "You know." When Steve still didn't understand Ron rolled his eyes in disgust. "The Kill List, you idiot. I swear, sometimes you're dumber than a bag of wet mice."

Steve flushed but didn't say anything.

Jeff looked down at the paper in his hands. "Right you are. This is the order I want to go."

"Well?" Ron licked his lips. "Read it off."

"Okay. Swenson, Hood, Evan, Shane, Aaron, and Ross." Jeff watched them. When none of the boys responded he added. "But we can change up the order."

"Why them?" Steve asked.

Jeff sighed. "Swenson because he's ineffectual. Hood because she'd like to keep the girls locked up like nuns. Evan because he's dying anyway. It'd be a mercy killing. You saw him. Shane, Ross, and Aaron because we have to thin out the competition a little."

"Competition for the girls?" Ron shrugged. "I'm not interested in them. Why not have Leeds on the list then? He's an asshole and he's constantly chasing the girls."

"I kinda like Ross. He helped me with my homework," Steve added.

Jeff crossed off Ross' name and added Leeds. "So, Swenson, Hood, Evan, Shane, Aaron, and Leeds."

"In that order?" Ron shook his head. "It should be Swenson, Leeds, Hood, and Evan. Then reassess. We'll see how they all react. I mean, Shin might freak the fuck out."

"He's a good guard, though. And he likes cleaning up. He knows how to fix things. He's useful."

"What about Pria and Maya? It's not like any of us are going to go for them. I mean, they're Indian." Steve stood and stretched.

"I don't know. Put a bag of their heads. They're still a good sperm bank." Jeff grinned as the rest laughed at his crude remark. In truth, though, he thought both Pria and Maya were very pretty.

"So, Swenson, Leeds, Hood, Evan. In that order?" Ron nodded. "Though, if Shane or Aaron present themselves as good targets…" He let the thought hang in the air.

Caleb, who had been quiet throughout the whole conversation, closed his book. "We're really going to do it? Kill people? Murder them?"

Jeff renumbered the list. "Yes. For the good of the academy. You want to survive the winter, don't you? Or would you rather starve?" His eyes narrowed at the thought. "Or are you the one stealing the food?"

Caleb shook his head. "Not stealing and no, I don't want to starve. But we're talking about killing people. I just...I've never killed anyone. Not even a zombie."

Jeff swallowed hard in sudden remembrance of the few he's had to kill. Don't think about her, he ordered himself as he clenched a fist. "You're lucky. I don't ever want to have to fight zombies again. That's why we're doing this. So we'll survive and be safe." His eyes hardened. "And we're starting with Swenson. Going to make it look like suicide."

Ron stood, moved to stand next to Jeff, and looked down at Caleb then over at Steve. "Are you with us or not?"

Steve hesitated before he stepped to Jeff's other side. "Yeah. Are you with us or not?" His voice wasn't as strong as Ron's.

Caleb froze and flushed for a moment before he grinned wide, baring his teeth. "Don't get your panties in a wad." He stood. "I just wanted to make sure you all understood what you were saying. I'm in. I'm with you."

Jeff nodded. "Good. So, here's what we're going to do with Swenson..."

* * *

Evan sat across from his dog, watching it uselessly claw at the equipment cage. Beauregard was attacking the hinge side of the door because that was as far as he could reach. The chain bolted to the wall stopped him from attacking the latched side. He was sure Beau would be able to escape if he could run full on at the door. If he threw himself at the door enough times the latch would give.

Standing on partially numbed feet, with his joints screaming their pain, Evan crossed close to the metal mesh cage. He considered the bolt in the wall and the zombie dog before him.

He could see that Beau had already pulled one of the bolts free from the wall and it really was only a matter of time before the other bolt came free. He looked around for a wrench and found it in a pile of other tools.

"Well, Beau. If I'm going to join the winning team I'm going to do it all the way."

Evan started to put the wrench through the mesh to loosen the bolt but Beau attacked the wrench as soon as it was part way through the small opening. Evan yanked the wrench back out and considered things for a moment.

Moving his left hand away from him he put it on the mesh of the equipment return slot. "Good boy," Evan crooned. "Good boy. You want a bite, you're going to get a bite." Slowly unlocking and lifting the return slot door he waited until Beau moved away from the wall to slide the wrench back in. All he needed was a couple of good turns to get the bolt loose.

He let the slot door close with a clack. Beau moved to just beneath it. Evan opened the slot door again and dropped it as he turned the bolt another quarter turn. The third time he opened the equipment return slot, Beauregard lunged at the door and Evan's hand. The bolt in the wall strained and popped free.

"Good boy, Beau. Good boy!" Evan couldn't keep the elation out of his voice. He dropped the wrench and took a breath as Beau shifted to directly under the equipment return panel, the chain around his neck and attached to his harness dragging on the floor in a musical jingle.

Using his right hand to slowly open the panel, Evan thrust his left hand in and managed to pet his beloved dog twice before Beauregard snarled and savaged his hand, tearing the flesh off it and shaking it back and forth.

Evan cried out. It hurt more than he thought it would. He struggled against his dog, yanking his arm through the slot and slamming it shut. He sank to the floor, cradling his wounded, bleeding hand to his chest as he gasped in sobs, tears streaming down his face. Looking down, he saw that he was missing a finger and part of his palm. "Good boy," he whispered. "Good boy. Soon, I won't be feeling anything anymore."

Slumping with his back to the cage Evan felt his dog's renewed attack on the door. Evan reached over his head and unlocked it. He stayed that way, with his back against the door, feeling every jarring attack. He felt the door's latch pop and knew that he, his body weight, was the only thing keeping Beauregard trapped.

Evan knew that wouldn't last long and wondered who would be the first to find them. Then they could all join the winning team together.

* * *

Nancy and Kimberly watched Sophia and Athena leave the nurse's office. The two women were quiet for a long time. Finally, Nancy spoke. "We need to do something about this. If Principal Swenson isn't going to help we need to deal with it."

Kimberly nodded. "Yes."

"Permanently."

"Yes."

"Do you have any ideas?"

The younger woman paused and then nodded. "Yes. I think I have one. But I'm going to need your help."

Nancy tilted her head. "Whatever you need. What are you going to do?"

"I'm going to offer him me…and a whole lot more." Kimberly waved a hand. "I don't have the plan worked out. Let me sleep on it. I have an idea. Plus, I need to lock down Bonny Hall. I mean really lock it down. I'd feel a lot more comfortable if you shifted as much as you can from here to a makeshift infirmary in Bonny Hall."

"And if one of the boys or faculty is hurt and needs help?"

"We'll deal with it on a case by case basis. At least in the short term. At least until I've neutered Leeds."

The older woman nodded. "I can do that."

* * *

"Sir, I'm sorry to bother you this late but I've found something you need to see." Jeff stood in the doorway of Swenson's suite and waited as the principal regarded him.

"Can't it wait until morning?" Robert didn't bother to hide his irritation at being interrupted. He was already angry with Jeff and didn't want to leave the comfort of his rooms. He had just gotten them warm enough and leaving now meant the fire could, probably would, go out.

The boy shook his head. "I'm sorry, sir, it really can't. I wouldn't have woken you if I hadn't found…" He paused. "It's best if I just show you. You'll need your coat. It's in the main hall."

Robert looked at him a moment longer, then sighed. "You're not going away until I come with you, are you." It was a statement rather than a question, born of experience. The boy was not one of the youngest Eagle Scouts in the tri-cities for nothing. It was his dogged determination and persistence that made Jeff so valuable.

"No, sir. I'm not. You really need to see this."

The principal got his coat and bundled up. This late in the year the evenings were cold. Without a word the two of them left Hadfield Hall for the Main Hall. Robert shivered. Ever since the Outbreak he didn't like to go out at night. Light could be seen from a long way away by anyone and everything. Once they were inside the Main Hall Jeff spoke up again.

"I was in the attic, looking to see what we had that could be used to its best advantage and…"

"This building has an attic?" Robert eyed the barely seen boy as they walked down the hallway and to the staircase. "How'd you find that out?"

Jeff was quiet for a moment, "When we locked down the campus I went through all of the buildings I could from top to bottom to see what could be useful. I mean, I didn't examine every single one thoroughly but I did keep track of the rooms I found to go back and examine later. Today I decided that I should really go through the attic of this building since I hadn't…and, well…you never know what you'll find stashed away in an attic.

Robert eyed the back of Jeff's head. *His story sounds like something he's practiced,* the principal thought. *Either what he found is really good, really dangerous, or really bad.* "What did you find? I don't want to play a guessing game with you. Just tell me."

"It's really better if you see it for yourself."

This time, the principal could hear the joy in the boy's tone. It must be good and possibly dangerous. The two were not mutually exclusive. "Fine."

The two of them didn't say another word until they reached the top floor and Jeff led them to a closet that turned out to be part closet and part hidden passageway. Robert watched with wonder as Jeff pulled a latch that revealed a pull-down staircase. "After you, sir. I'll need to close it after us. The lights will come on when I close the stairs."

Robert climbed the stairs into darkness, pausing momentarily to look down and ask. "Lights?" Just after he crested the floor and was halfway into the black room, something looped itself around his neck and yanked him off balance. He gave a strangled cry as he fell over and was dragged into the room by his neck.

* * *

Shin watched the flickering lights move across the quad to the Main Hall. He saw the lights move through the building, up to the fourth floor, then disappear. Considering this for a long moment he nodded to himself and bundled up. He followed the same path as the lights in the dark. He knew the campus ground so well that he had no need of light.

PLAN
FOR
SUCCESS

CHAPTER
SIX

After the metal side door in the eight foot stone wall of the Salton Academy closed and locked with a too-loud sound the four teenagers stood there for a moment, looking between themselves and the dangerous wild land of *outside*. Lee readjusted his pack and squared his shoulders. "All right. Let's go. Me and Melissa up front. Nicholas and Joe in back. Watch for movement like we discussed. We'll stop at the twenty minute mark and do the radio check. I want to be at the coffee stand by then."

The four of them walked quickly and quietly through the empty grounds of Salton Academy property. The academy owned far more land than was within the safety of the walls because of Gregory Salton's bequeathment. It had come with the stipulation that any of the land not used for the academy would be allowed to remain natural and undisturbed.

This made the walk both easier and harder. There was one main, little-used road to follow. It was lined with rolling hills and denuded trees. They would see any zombies coming but it also meant that there would be no place to hide. All of them felt exposed. By tacit, unspoken agreement, all of them had unsheathed their blunt weapons: baseball bats for Lee and Joe, a cricket bat for Nicholas, and a field hockey stick for Melissa.

A mile and a half later, when they crested the last hill and saw the small drive through coffee stand, there was a collective sigh of relief with the loosing of shoulders and other tensed muscles. But no one broke ranks and Lee signaled a slowdown of pace. Everyone watched for signs of movement. Just because the coffee stand had been cleared before didn't mean it was still clear.

Nothing moved but them.

When they arrived at the coffee stand door, Lee motioned for Melissa to open the door as he readied his baseball bat. She opened it in a rush and Lee moved in but the interior was empty.

"This is going to suck," Melissa said as Lee lowered his bat.

He looked at his watch. "Yeah. It is. But, we can do it. And it's time for the radio check."

The four of them crowded into the small building, not wanting to be left outside, feeling so exposed. It was just big enough to fit all of them in single line.

Lee put the radio earpiece in, turned on the radio and spoke. "Salton Academy, this is Supply Team. Over. Yeah, we got it. Over." Lee's face went from neutral to disbelieving to rage as he listened to the radio. The other teens looked at each other, concerned. "You've got to be kidding me. Over. I swear to God, Jeff, when we get back, I'm going to stick my boot so far up your ass you'll be spiting laces for the rest of your miserable life. Over. I will kill you myself!"

Lee's face was red as he snarled incoherently. He yanked the earbud from his ear and looked like he was to throw the radio or the earbud into the wall. No one moved or said anything while he fought for control of his considerable temper. With an exhale of breath that was more growl than sigh, Lee put the radio and earbud away with careful, precise, controlled movements. He took another breath and looked at his pale-faced friends. "We've got a problem."

"I can see that." Nicholas shifted his pack and put it on the floor. "So…what's the deal?"

Lee looked from Melissa to Nicholas to Joe. "That sonofabitch has declared that unless we get everything on his tier one list, he's not going to let us back into the school."

"What?" Melissa shook her head, her look of shock mirroring the rest.

"He can't do that!" Joe clenched his fists.

Nicholas didn't say anything. Instead, he hunkered down and pulled the lists from his backpack.

"He can. He did." Lee shook his head. "I don't know how he's going to enforce it but that's the situation."

"What about Shin?" Melissa looked at them all. "Didn't he say he'd let us in whether or not he had permission? Do you think he knew this was going to happen?"

Lee shrugged. "I don't know. But Shin is an option. The thing is, Jeff also said that if we didn't get everything on that list the academy wouldn't survive the winter. Maybe this is his way of motivating us?" He took a couple more breaths, calming himself and thinking as hard as he could.

"Piss poor way of doing so." Joe shook his head. "This changes everything."

"Does it?" Nicholas stood, still looking at the list. "Tier one has nothing but staples: flour, baking powder, rice, salt, beans. Just a lot of it. I mean, I think we can get everything on the tier one list with no problem except bringing it back. It's about fifty pounds apiece if we only get the staples."

Joe sheathed his bat and took out his 9mm Smith and Wesson pistol. He checked it and the magazine. Then he checked the other two magazines. "I don't trust that guy. I never have. Too high and mighty." He nodded to the rest. "Check your weapons. Make sure he didn't short you in the name of conserving resources."

Nicholas shook his head. "I don't think he would."

"I do." Joe cut him off and held his pistol. "This weapon was mine. My personal gun. The only reason I let Shin put it in the armory with the rest of the hunting rifles and personal pistols is because I trust Shin. I trust him not to let idiots get firearms. But…" He pulled a second, smaller gun—an Airweight Smith and Wesson snubnose .38 special—from his pocket. "But I didn't give him everything. I'm betting other kids didn't either."

Lee nodded. "I'm sure Jeff kept something himself."

"So, what are we going to do?" Melissa frowned, her brows furrowed. "Get the stuff and go back like nothing happened?"

"No. Yes." Lee paused, still working to control his urge to kick something. "We're going to follow the plan for now. But when we get back there will be a reckoning. I don't know why he made the threat but I'm not going to let that stand. Everyone will know."

The four of them nodded to each other in agreement.

"All right. Things haven't changed. We still need to get supplies." Nicholas put the list of needed supplies away. "As planned, we walk until we make it to the burned out city, then we make camp and forage from there. Lee leads. We follow."

Everyone looked at Lee for his confirmation. His flush had faded but his lips were pressed into a thin, white line of anger. He took in a deep breath and nodded as he exhaled. "As planned. Walk until dark or we hit the city. Keep conversation to a minimum and keep alert for all dangers, not just zombies. Wild animals and feral people."

* * *

The day passed quickly with no incident beyond the heart-stopping raucous of disturbed birds. There was little to break up the scenery of the road except for the occasional farmhouse in the distance. All of them picked up their pace once they recognized the final hill before the road plunged into the valley that housed the burned out city.

At the top of the hill the four of them stopped and stared. Below them was the spread of civilization that meant death with its low rise apartment and business buildings, tracks of cloned homes in neat rows, and a large strip mall. About two-thirds of the city looked blackened and broken. More than one water tower had fallen. Also, while there was no visible flame, the scent of burnt rubble reached them even up here, miles away.

"Maybe my idea wasn't so good," Melissa said, her voice soft and disappointed.

Lee took her hand and squeezed it. "No, it's fine. Most people would avoid this place, assuming that the fire would've destroyed everything."

"Yeah," Joe added. "It doesn't look that bad. There's lots of buildings still standing. Lots to forage in."

"And lots of places to hide." Nicholas's voice was as soft as Melissa's.

She glanced at them and smiled.

Lee let go of her hand and readjusted his pack. "Let's take that house there for the night. We'll make the city in the morning, fresh and ready for everything."

* * *

Principal Robert Swenson could not scream as he was dragged off his feet. The rope around his neck was tight and the fall knocked the wind from him. All he could do was scrabble for the rope at his throat and be placed where his attackers wanted him. He didn't know who was doing the attacking but, because Jeff wasn't rushing to his aid, he knew the boy was in on it. Once again he was betrayed by someone he thought would never stoop so low.

"We have him." The voice was behind Robert as he was dragged to his feet by his neck. He recognized it. Ronald… something. His body was too busy trying to get air into his lungs to make his brain work.

Jeff came up the staircase and into the attic. He held his flashlight pointed up, illuminating the room. He bent over and pulled the folding staircase closed before he smiled at the principal. It was not a nice smile. Jeff looked around. "Lanterns."

Two camp lanterns were flicked on, allowing Robert to see all of his assailants in the low light as he twisted around. His heart sank but he wasn't surprised. Caleb and Steve stood together. Ron was behind him, manning the rope. Looking up, Robert saw that the rope around his neck was tossed over one of the roof's main support beams. His hands told him that they had even fashioned an executioner's knot that would not slip when they hanged him.

"What are you doing?" Robert could not hide the fear in his raspy voice as he looked around. "Why are you doing this to me?" His fingers continued to scrabble at the noose around his neck, trying to get some purchase.

Jeff gave him a withering look. "You suck as a principal and as a leader. If we left you in charge you'd kill us all."

"I do not. I would not!" Robert twisted around as Ron pulled more on the rope, making him stand on tiptoe. Robert had not realized the tall, slender boy was so strong. "I saved us. I kept the zombies out. I made sure we were safe." He begged the boys with his eyes and his words even though he knew it wouldn't help. A line had been crossed that could not be uncrossed.

"Wrong." Jeff's voice was full of venom. "You left a zombie inside the walls. You didn't do anything other than order the campus closed. We did the rest. Hell, if I didn't tell you, you wouldn't have known about the food problem. You just sat behind your desk, pretending to work when there's nothing for you to work on. You don't have lists or plans for the next few weeks preparing us for the coming snow. You haven't even asked about the woodpile or started making arrangements to conserve heat in the dorms. You have no idea how to survive. You're just a parasite."

Robert stared at him for a moment. "I can change. I can shift my focus. I can do this. I can be the leader you want me to be."

"Too late." It was Ron who spoke now. "We already have the leader we need to survive the winter and the zombies. You aren't it."

Jeff smiled at that and at the nodding heads of Steve and Caleb. "My men have spoken. You aren't needed and we don't want you." He gestured to Steve and Caleb. Both boys joined Ron. "Any last words, Principal Swenson?"

Robert didn't get to say any of the things he wanted to say—*I hope they eat you* or *you all are getting the leader you deserve* or even the simple *go to hell*—because the boys manning the rope all pulled at once and he had no air to give voice to his last curses.

Jeff watched how far up they dragged the man. At the correct height, he called, "Stop. Tie it off." They did as they were told and then joined Jeff in watching their former principal choke to death. For a long while, longer than Jeff would have thought possible, the only sound in the room was Swenson's gagging, gasping attempts to get air. Then even those went silent as his body continued to jerk and twitch in futile gestures to get free.

Finally, after a good sixty seconds of utter stillness, Caleb asked, "Is he…?" His voice was soft and he sounded like he was going to get sick.

Jeff looked at Caleb. His friend's face was as white as Swenson's was purple. "Yes. I think so." For a moment, Jeff couldn't move. Then he forced himself to. If he was going to be the one to make hard decisions, the ones that would save them all, his actions needed to speak as loud as his words. He stepped forward, reached out, and took Swenson's still warm wrist in hand. Jeff carefully felt around for a pulse. Nothing. He tried the other wrist. Nothing. He grinned as he looked up, suddenly elated. "He's dead, Jim."

Ron gave a whoop of excitement and the rest of them joined in with their own shouts of relief and adrenaline. They pounded each other on the back and grinned until Jeff motioned them for calm. "Okay. We gotta go. We gotta get back to Hadfield. Get the lanterns. Flashlights only. If you need them."

The lights were extinguished as Jeff opened the folding staircase. They trooped out of the attic, turning off all but one flashlight as they went. Much more subdued now that they were in the hallway Steve asked in a whisper, "Swenson's not going to, you know, *turn*, is he?"

Jeff shook his head and answered in that same quiet whisper. "No. I'll come back and check in a week if Shin hasn't found him in his rounds."

"You think Shin's going to find him?"

"I'm counting on it. He patrols every floor of every building almost every single day. It's what makes him so good at his job. He'll find Swenson, assume it was suicide, and that will be that."

Ron paused at the stairway door. "And if he doesn't?"

Jeff shrugged. "We deal with it."

* * *

Shin made his way from Hadfield Hall to the admin building. He kept to the shadows of the building as he did so. He did not believe that those already within would be looking out the window but one could never be too careful. After three months of survival, pretending things would be okay, everyone was beginning to realize deep within they would not be. Things were coming to a boiling point.

He headed up to top floor of the admin building, taking care to be as silent as possible. The last place he saw the flashlights was at the end of the hallway where the attic access was. He tried to think of what could be in the attic that boys felt they needed to come here in the middle of the night. Nothing came to mind.

The folding staircase was closed.

Shin tucked himself into the shadows just inside one of the unused classrooms and failed to suppress a shiver at its chill. Winter would be early this year. The Salton Academy might see snow for Christmas. Probably before. He made a mental note to shore up the drafty spots in his room. There was a noise from above. It sounded like faint shouts of triumph. Whatever the students were doing they had chosen well. Sound did not carry from the attic and there were few windows.

Shin froze where he was as the folding attic staircase lowered itself and the boys came down it with careful steps, using only one flashlight to guide their way. He listened in mute horror to their plans. Shin realized that not only had the four students murdered the principal, they were ready to murder him—if he did not act as they expected him to act.

Waiting until the last sounds of the boys disappeared from the empty building Shin moved to glance out the classroom window. He was relieved to see the flicking shadows of the students and surprised to see that they did not use the flashlight outside. It was something to note for the future.

He turned back to the attic access and unfolded the staircase, not wanting to see, but needing to see, what the boys had done to the principal. Poking his head above the floor of the attic he clicked on his smallest flashlight and scanned the room. The principal's body was front and center, hanging still.

Shin considered the scene and the perpetrators. He made a decision. He did not like what had happened but he was not willing to challenge the boys. At least, not yet. He couldn't be sure they wouldn't suddenly rampage and kill more of the students. For the moment the boys needed to feel safe and undetected. Shin needed to figure out how to deal with four healthy teenagers willing to kill without being murdered himself.

Shin looked around, then entered the attic fully. He picked up the low stool that the boys intended to use as Principal Swenson's means of getting up high enough to kick over and commit suicide. It seemed they had forgotten about this small fact in their triumph.

He moved the stool to just under the principal's feet, then carefully tipped it over and set it on its side. He slid it forward a couple of inches to make it look like the principal had kicked it. Stepping back, Shin examined the scene, nodded, and left the attic. Tomorrow he would get Nurse Krenshaw and have her announce the man's death.

CHAPTER
SEVEN

Give me one good reason we should go back." Joe looked around at his friends and fellow scavengers as they sat around the kitchen table eating stale pop tarts and dry cereal. "Seriously. Give me a reason we should go back and live with that asshole."

For a moment no one spoke. Then Melissa, looking at the rosy pre-dawn light through the kitchen window, shrugged. "Because we promised. Just because Jeff's an ass doesn't mean we need to be. If we don't go back with the supplies they might not make it through the winter."

Nicholas nodded. "Also, where are we going to stay?" He gestured to the house they'd taken over. "This place is nice but it's not indefensible. In fact, it's an open invitation to be eaten if we tried to settle it and grow food and stuff."

"We haven't see any zombies yet." Joe shook his head. "I read that zombies shouldn't be able to last as long as they supposedly do because of all of the carrion eaters in the world."

Now Lee looked up from his food. "No. We don't think like that. We can't. If we do, we're dead."

"You can't honestly want to go back to the academy after what Jeff did." Joe paused. "Can you? You were so damn mad…"

Lee pushed away his empty bowl and started in on his pop tarts. "Don't be so hard on Jeff. Yeah. I was mad. I still am. But I get him. I understand why he's doing this. At least I hope I understand why."

Melissa tilted her head. "What happened to him to make him like this? Do you know?"

Lee didn't answer for a long time. Just took large bites of the sweet, stale pastry, chewed, and swallowed. He looked off in the distance as he marshaled his thoughts. "You know our rules: Always assume there's a zombie behind every door. Weapons at the ready. Stay as quiet as possible. No injured left behind, only dead. And no one goes home. You ever wonder why that last?"

Nicholas nodded. "I always thought it was because it would be too dangerous to fixate on one point."

Lee looked at him. "No. It's because you may find who you're looking for and they may try to eat you."

Melissa, Nicholas, and Joe looked at each other, swallowing hard. Melissa pushed her food away. Joe frowned. "Did…is that what happened to Jeff?"

"Yeah. On the first supply run." Lee pushed the debris of his breakfast towards the center of the table. "He said we should go to his house because they were prepared for emergencies. Had a stockpile of food and stuff. And they did. Except…his mom was there, too. He had to kill her." Lee sighed, looking to the side.

"And, his sister. She was upstairs in her bedroom. Dead. She'd left Jeff a note and killed herself with sleeping pills. If we'd been there a couple days earlier, she would've been alive."

"How?" Nicholas's voice was soft with understanding and horror.

Lee shrugged. "They all prepared in that family. Mormon, you know. It's part of their thing or something. Kristi, that was her name, had supplies in her room. She'd locked herself in and waited for her big brother to come save her while her mom roamed the house, trying to get to her. She was stuck. She ran out of food and hope. We found her curled up in her bed, asleep-like, with the letter addressed to Jeff in her hand."

"What'd it say?" Melissa leaned forward.

"Don't know. He wouldn't show me and I didn't push it."

Nicholas and Joe exchanged a glance. "Damn," Joe muttered.

They were silent for a long time as the sun continued to rise, shining rays of golden light onto the kitchen wall. Melissa shivered. Lee stood with a purpose, pushing back his chair. "Time to forage. We got supplies to gather."

The rest stood with him, quietly cleaning up and packing for the day's work.

* * *

Athena smiled, feeling more than a bit rebellious as she knocked on Evan's door. Mrs. Hood had declared that all of the girls needed to use the buddy system because of Professor Leeds but she didn't say that the buddy needed to be another girl. Yes, that had been implied, but as the world had pretty much ended she felt justified in using the loophole. Besides, she liked Evan. A lot. Eventually he was going to realize it. She smiled, knocking again.

Her smile faded as Evan didn't answer. Athena's heart beat faster as the fear took over. What if he was hurt? What if the medicine had stopped working. What if…the worst had come? Her cynical mind cut through the panic: What if he was just sleeping?

"Evan?" Her voice was soft despite her suppressed fear. She tried the door and found it unlocked. Stepping in she called his name again. "Evan?"

The room was immaculate. The bed was made, the floor clean of dirty clothes, everything on his desk was put away in its proper place. Evan was not here. The only thing that stood out was the sheet of paper placed in the middle of the desk. Athena stepped to the desk and looked down at the paper filled with Evan's cramped handwriting. She picked the paper up as she read the opening line.

Dear Principal Swenson,

It's been so long since we've really talked that I don't know how to start this letter. So I'm starting it like this. We both know that I'm dying. We both know there's nothing to be done about it. I have, maybe, three months left. A month of half meds and two months of no meds. For those two months, right in the heart of winter, I will be unable to move without soul shattering pain, without my skin erupting in giant welts of open sores and flaking skin, without the comfort of either of my parents.

You took me away from mom because you are selfish. You stay away from me because you are weak and ashamed of what your son has become. For this, I will not forgive you. However, as you are my father, and I do love you—despite everything—I want you to know what I do now I do of my own free will. It is not because of you. It is because I think it's the best thing I can do for myself now.

I'm going to go join the winning team. Soon there will be two zombies for you to deal with: Beauregard and me. Treat me as you will. Put me down or chain me up. I have no opinion either way. I will be like Beau. I will feel no pain, no joy, no love, no hate. I will feel nothing except the urge to feed. Right now, that idea seems like heaven.

Live well, Father. I'm sorry I wasn't good enough for you.

Sincerely,
Evan

P.S. Tell Athena I loved her and have appreciated everything she'd tried to do for me.

Athena dropped the suicide note from nerveless fingers. She covered her mouth with both hands, murmuring, "No, no, no, no," into them. She stared at the paper, not able to think of what to do next. A train wreck of immediate thoughts crashed within her mind. She had to tell Principal Swenson. She had to raise the alarm. She had to get Nurse Krenshaw. She had to stop Evan from killing himself.

It was this last thought that galvanized her into action. She might be able to stop Evan before it was too late. Turning from the desk Athena ran from Evan's room, closing the door behind her. The wind of the door's movement pushed the paper off the desk and onto the floor where it half hid itself under the bed.

* * *

Shin bowed his head as he watched Nurse Krenshaw examine Robert Swenson's hanging body with the air of a woman who has seen this before. He tried to think if there had ever been a suicide at the Salton Academy. Vaguely, he remembered training about such things and an example of what to do, how to protect the student's reputation, and the school's reputation. There must have been but that would have happened before he was hired on. Nurse Krenshaw had at least a decade of service at the academy over him.

The nurse was tired. She had been awakened by Shin far too early for her liking. "Yes. Suicide." She picked up the kicked over stool and moved it as she shook her head. "I knew the man was a coward but I didn't think he'd have the balls for this." The old woman looked at Shin. "You don't look surprised."

"His son is dying." It was the only thing he could think to say.

The impassive look on Nurse Krenshaw's face softened. "Yes. I know." She looked up at the hanging body. "I know he added the boy's medicine to supply run list but no one really thinks they're going to be able to find it." She shook her head again. "That poor boy. First his medicine is running out and now this."

For a moment the two of them stood there in the dark silence of the attic with the body of the former Principal of the Salton Academy hanging between them. Then Nurse Krenshaw slid her professional mask in place. "Let's get him down."

Shin nodded and moved to where the rope was tied. "When will we tell the rest?" He worked on the expertly tied knot, loosening it while keeping a tight hold on the rope so the body didn't fall to the ground.

"Immediately. As soon as we…" She paused and thought for a moment. "After we package the body up. We'll leave it up here. Then we'll call a meeting. I don't want the children seeing us carrying the body before we tell them whose body it is and what happened. This will…cause ripples. I don't know what everyone will do. And I'm not sure who will step up to lead." She gave him a speculative look.

He slowly lowered the body to the floor before he said anything. "I would not lead. I believe Mrs. Hood would be the best choice but I fear that someone else will step up. This could cause a lot more problems."

Nurse Krenshaw gave him a sharp look and nodded. "Professor Leeds will believe he deserves the mantle."

The two of them arranged themselves around the body—Shin at the head, Krenshaw at the feet—then hefted him into the waiting body bag. It was not an easy thing to move dead weight but they managed with labored breaths and strong stomachs. When they were done Shin looked at the older woman. "I believe many will object to Professor Leeds taking the leadership role."

"You included?" This time, Nancy's look was considering.

He nodded once and said no more.

* * *

Athena burst into the gymnasium already shouting Evan's name. "Evan! Please! Evan, don't do it!" She ran through the basketball court as the door slammed behind her, then stopped before the door to the back hallway. Steeling herself, Athena opened it up and walked down the hallway. "Evan?"

Silently she prayed that he was all right, that he had just wanted to scare his father into some sort of response to show that the man still cared about his son. Her steps slowed. She didn't like coming here. She didn't like the zombie dog. But Evan had asked her to visit with the dog with him a couple of times. She had done so because she wanted to be with Evan.

Athena walked quietly down the hallway. "Evan? Please.

Evan, are you all right?" She listened, standing just outside the cracked doorway that opened into the equipment locker where the dog was. She could hear the dog snarling and keening. The sound made the hair on the back of her neck stand up. She wanted to run away. Then she heard a grunt. A human grunt. Evan. Her heart soared. He was still alive.

She burst into the backroom. "Evan, thank—oh, God!"

The zombie that was no longer Evan had just stood, allowing the dog its freedom. Even as she backpedaled with a scream, Beauregard, beloved of Evan, leaped for Athena and latched onto her warding arm. The two of them fell in a tumble into the hallway with Evan lurching after them.

Athena screamed and struggled as the zombie dog ripped chunks of flesh from her arm, swallowing them whole. Athena screamed as Evan ripped open the soft flesh of her abdomen with tearing fingers and questing teeth. Athena screamed as the zombies ate her alive.

Then Athena stopped screaming.

* * *

"Clear." Nicholas's voice was carried through the hallway of the ranch-style house without shouting.

"Clear." Melissa sounded relieved.

"Clear." Lee, as usual, sounded like he was shopping for groceries.

"Fuck!"

They turned as one toward Joe's implicit warning of zombies. Joe, at the end of the hall, had his baseball bat up as a barrier and was keeping the old man zombie at bay, but just barely. The zombie had hold of the bat and was lunging at Joe's face with snapping teeth as they wrestled. Lee and Melissa moved in, Lee swinging high as Melissa used her field hockey stick to hook one of the zombie's ankles. She yanked as hard as she could as Lee's bat connected with the zombie's head. The zombie fell backward, letting go of Joe's bat as a second zombie moved up.

This zombie was an old woman and much more decayed with a large dog collar around her neck. She shuffled forward, half falling over the old man as she grasped for living flesh. Joe hit her in the jaw, then moved back. The woman fell forward and struggled to get at Joe from her prone position, reaching for his leg. Lee and Joe both pounded the woman's head to mush.

"This one's still up!" Melissa moved back behind Lee and Joe, joining Nicholas who had taken up a guard position behind them. Joe got to his feet and moved in with Lee.

The old man shifted into a sitting position and was rewarded with two baseball bats to the head. With a soft groan the zombie flopped to the floor, his head caved in, and did not move again.

Lee turned to the last closed door and nodded to Joe. He opened up and Lee lunged forward to meet any new threats. After a moment of silence he called, "Clear." He motioned them inside. "Kitchen."

"Jesus. Why do I always get the zombie room?" Joe cleaned off his bat with a kitchen towel emblazoned with butterflies and kittens. Melissa and Lee shrugged as they cleaned their weapons of zombie gore.

"Not much here," Nicholas said, his head in the pantry. "There's two bags of unopened rice and one bag of flour. It looks like they cleaned things out."

"Better than nothing." Lee took one of the bags of rice as Joe put the flour in his backpack and Nicholas put the other bag of rice in his backpack.

"You realize that the old man didn't die all that long ago. And the old woman had died…probably in the Outbreak." Melissa looked at the refrigerator. There was a pair of heart magnet on it with the names "Angie" and "Cole" on it. "The pantry wasn't cleaned out so much as the old man, Cole, was living off of what he had left. Must've been taking care of Angie." The three teens looked at Melissa as if she'd sprouted another head. Melissa shrugged, pointing at the magnet. "Then Angie got loose and got Cole."

"Why the fuck…?" Joe looked green.

Lee gave him a half-smile. "I guess 'til death do you part' meant a little more to Cole once the Outbreak happened. More like 'til permanent death do you part.'"

Nicholas shook his head, looking as ill as Joe. "I didn't want to know their names. Never tell me their names. I don't want to know. I don't want to know who they were in life. I don't want to know who they were after we put them down. Don't do it."

"I'm sorry." Melissa ducked her head. "I didn't mean…I won't do it again."

Lee hugged her. "It's okay. It's just hard going through these houses." He looked at the other two. "But we gotta. It's better to work the fringes than try and move into a place that might have more zombies than we can handle."

"I know." Nicholas sighed. "I wish we were back at the academy. Even with that asshole."

Joe shrugged. "I agree. I wonder what they're doing now?"

"Who knows?" Nicholas looked out the kitchen window, watching the clouds obscure the afternoon sky. "Definitely having a better time that we are."

"C'mon." Lee let go of Melissa. "We still need to find another hundred and fifty pounds of staples before we can go home."

* * *

As the students filed into the Commons their chatter stuttered to a halt as all of the adults on campus stood with solemn faces in front of dining room. All the adults except for Principal Swenson. Nancy Krenshaw stood in the middle of them with Shin on her left and Kimberly on her right. Michael lounged against one of the pillars nearest Shin.

Nancy surveyed the students, counting them and coming up short by two…six if you counted the four students out scavenging for food and medical supplies. Counting the girls—Julie, Pria, Maya, Rose, Sophia, and Toni—told her who was missing. Melissa was gone and Athena wasn't present. That gave her the name of the other missing student. Evan. She wondered if he had found out somehow and the two of them were together.

Glancing left and right Nancy saw that both Kimberly and Shin had noticed the missing two. A longer look at Michael saw that he was staring at Sophia in open and undisguised anger. Sophia, for her part, was looking only at Kimberly. Nancy knew she had to help Kimberly with that situation and soon. Otherwise, Sophia might be in a lot of trouble.

As soon as all of the students were settled Nancy cleared her throat. "Students, it is my sad duty to inform you that Principal Swenson is dead. He committed suicide last night." She paused as the assembled erupted in a torrent of shocked whispers. Then she raised her voice. "We assembled you all here to tell you all at once so there are no rumors. Suicide is a terrible tragedy. The faculty is here to support you all. If you need help, let us know. If you want to talk to anyone, we are here for you."

Michael suddenly stood up straight. "Yes. We are here for your *comfort* and are willing to talk to any of you day or night."

While he addressed the students as a whole he put a particular stress on the word 'comfort' that everyone noticed…and noticed he looked at Sophia as he said it. Sophia paled but continued to look straight ahead at the dorm mistress.

Kimberly nodded and cut off anything else Michael was going to say. "Ladies, we will be meeting in my suite immediately after this meeting to discuss things."

"Where is Evan?" Jeff's voice rang out from the audience. "Is he okay?"

The adults looked at each other and shook their heads. Nancy took a breath. "We suspect he is with Athena right now. His father may have left him a note or something. He may already know and is grieving in private. However, as soon as any of you find Athena or Evan, tell them that I would like to speak to both of them."

There was another moment of silence. Then Jeff stood. "Will we be having a service for Principal Swenson? If yes…when?"

Nancy nodded. "We will. I need to consult with Shin on the burial and other such details."

Shin nodded to Nancy and then to Jeff. He kept his face impassive.

"I'd like to help. If that's okay." Jeff's voice sounded small, almost pleading.

Michael nodded. "Of course. Of course. We can talk about back at Hadfield. I think Kim—Mrs. Hood has the right of it. Gentlemen, we'll have a meeting in the common room to talk more about things after this meeting is done."

"I think this is a good time to do that," Nancy said. "Once we have more answers, we'll let you all know. Meeting adjourned."

* * *

Jeff smiled to himself all the way back to Hadfield Hall. His plan had worked perfectly. None of the faculty suspected anything. Not even 'the Harridan' as Leeds liked to call her. Watching them subtly jockey for the leadership was interesting but not unexpected. He looked at the back of Professor Leeds' head and wondered just how easy he would be to manipulate until he and the boys decided to off him.

Jeff gave a sidelong glance at Ron. The other boy offered a knowing smile. Jeff couldn't help but smile back. Soon everything would be all right again. No one would starve. Everyone would survive the winter. Everyone he wanted to survive that is.

CHAPTER
EIGHT

Melissa held up her hand in a fist, silently halting the group. She looked around the cul-de-sac they had targeted for savaging and sniffed the air. The boys looked at her and each other, then looked around, trying to catch whatever scent had caught Melissa's attention. She sniffed more and turned to the left, and took three steps in that direction. The boys stayed put, looking all around them, nervous to be out in the open.

Then Melissa pointed to the first house on the left. "Baby powder."

Lee came up beside her. "What?"

"I smell baby powder. Fresh. And cleanser, like baby wipes. We used to use them for sponge baths when we were camping and didn't care if the wildlife could scent you." She continued to point at the first house. "And look. Windows boarded up. I think we have survivors."

Nicholas and Joe came up next to them. They looked around at the rest of the houses. "Not boarded up," Joe murmured. "Now what?"

Lee shrugged. "We knock like civilized people."

"Knock?" Joe looked alarmed. "What if...?"

"...they try to kill us?" Again, Lee shrugged. "Been there. Done that. Can't smell the baby powder but I trust Mel's nose. If they're cleaning themselves with baby wipes they can't be all bad. You know?"

Joe shook his head. "No. I don't know. When the hell do baby wipes equal civilized people?"

"Makes a weird sort of sense to me." Nicholas rubbed the back of his neck.

Melissa tilted her head. "Can't hurt...well, it can. But I don't think it will."

She walked to the front door of the first house and knocked with the rest on her heel. She rapped three times and waited. They all heard the soft sound of movement, then silence. Melissa waited for a count of twenty, then knocked again. This time there was movement and the sounds of locks unlocking and furniture being moved.

The door opened and two wide-eyed, familiar, girls stood there looking at them. No one moved for a long moment. One girl had long red hair and pale skin. The other girl was tall with short black hair and dark skin.

"Heather?" Joe asked, not believing what he was seeing.

"Rachel." Nicholas whispered her name like a prayer.

Rachel and Heather looked at each other and burst into tears.

* * *

Michael stood to one side of the Hadfield common room and looked at the group of boys as they arranged themselves before him. No one sat down. Most likely because he had not sat. Good cue. After a moment of silence and hesitation Michael cleared his throat. "Look. I'm not going to beat around the bush here. Swenson's death is a damn shame but that doesn't mean he has to take us with him. We're strong enough to go on. As such, chores will go on, rotated by week with the exception of Jeff. He's permanent cook. But his helpers will continue to rotate."

He paused and looked around the room at the sea of solemn faces. There seemed to be too many and too little of them at the same time. He hadn't really cared too much about the upkeep of the dorm as long as it was done and he knew what he was doing. "Jeff..."

"Yes, sir?"

The boy's voice was respectful but his eyes were wary. Michael knew he needed to make friend of the boy as soon as he could. "You keep on top of the chore rotation, right?"

"Yes, sir."

"Keep doing that and get a helper." He looked around the group of boys and picked out the two quietest and youngest that he knew Jeff could boss around. "Ken and John, why don't you two help him out." The two boys looked at each other, then at Jeff. No one said anything. Michael took that as assent. "Good. If there's a problem, let me know. Otherwise I'm going to consider no news as good news."

Jeff nodded and shifted next to his newly assigned helpers. "Yes, sir."

Michael looked around again. "Anyone got any ideas on where Evan is?" He paused and gave them all a knowing smile. "Or where Evan would go with a girl?" There were some mutters and shaking of heads as well as some smirks. "Right. If you see him, let me know and let him know I want to talk to him. But no pressure. When he's ready. If he's grieving I'm happy to let him do it in the arms of his girl." He looked around. "Anything else? No? Dismissed."

The boys filtered out and up to their rooms. Michael watched them go, feeling pleased with himself for the impromptu speech. He turned towards his suite and paused. Shin was standing a respectful distance away. "Something, Mr. Yoshida?"

"May I walk you to your suite?" Shin kept his voice as respectful and as diffident as always.

Michael looked at the small man and his guard uniform and nodded. "All right. What's up?"

Shin walked beside him the short way down the faculty hallway. "I think we should consider what it will take to turn the common room into a common sleep area for the winter."

"Why?" Michael frowned at the idea.

"It will conserve on wood and, with the hanging of blankets, we can make sure we have one room that does not get cold. Cold students are sick students."

Michael opened his suite door and nodded. "Smart. Tell Jeff…" He paused as Shin shook his head. "What?"

"I am not their leader. They must see that you are thinking of them."

The engineering professor gave a sigh. "You're right and they'll need my skills to help them. Okay. I'll get on that. Anything else?"

Shin shook his head. "No."

"You going patrolling?"

"Yes."

Michael rubbed his chin. "Would you give the grounds an extra good search? Not just the perimeter? I don't like to think of the kids out in the woods, hurt. Grieving kids do stupid things."

Shin nodded. "Of course. It will take me most of the day."

"Fine. Fine. Just come by when you're done." Michael ducked into his suite, pleased with himself. The guard would leave him alone for at least the day while he did his woods search.

* * *

Nancy and Kimberly watched the girls leave the suite in pairs: Toni and Rose, Julie and Sophia, Pria and Maya. No one looked happy. All of them knew this transition could lead to problems. The biggest problem in the women's mind right now was Michael Leeds and his bold threat to Sophia in front of God and everyone.

"You wouldn't happen to have something that could kill a grown man, would you?" Kimberly hadn't realized she was going to asked the question until it came out of her mouth.

Nancy took the time to close the door before she answered. "You mean like morphine?"

The black woman's eyes went wide. "You have morphine?"

The nurse nodded. "And other sedatives that could put a man to sleep first before injecting him with a lethal dose." Nancy walked back to Kimberly and stood before her. "Are we really having this conversation?"

Kimberly knew it for the challenge it was: *are you really ready to kill a man?* Yes, she was. "Yes." The word echoing her thoughts. "Especially if that man is a clear danger to my girls."

Nancy gave her a long, penetrating look. Kimberly did not flinch or look away. Finally, the nurse nodded. "All right. Let's figure this out."

* * *

Melissa herded everyone inside to continue to the tearful reunion. Nicholas and Rachel held onto each other like they would never let go. Heather and Joe sat close enough together that it was clear something had been going on between them before the outbreak. As soon as everyone was seated Melissa asked whatever wanted to know. "Why happened? Why are you here?"

Heather and Rachel looked at each other and Rachel nodded to Heather to speak. "Rae and Gina were over at my house for summer break. My parents were gone to Italy. When everything happened Gina didn't wait. She told us we had to come here. That Todd and Sheena had a plan for this very thing. Sheena was on the field hockey team with us."

"I know Sheena but not Todd." Melissa looked around the living room. It looked like a normal house except for the boarded up windows. There were knickknacks on the shelves and discarded books on the table.

"He graduated last year." Lee nodded. "Good guy. Little strange, but I guess not as strange as I thought. Where are they, Sheena and Todd? And Gina?"

Heather shrugged a little. "I don't know. They left us a note. We didn't get here in time. I know they had an apocalypse plan. For all I know they're in Montana. That's where he's from. But they didn't say where they were going."

"Gina…didn't come back from foraging. That was about a month ago." Heather's voice was quiet. Joe reached out and squeezed her hand.

"We're guessing she got bit."

"So, where is everyone else?" Lee shifted in the recliner. "I really expected a lot more zombies."

Heather smiled a bitter smile. "That's because of the evac. The government evac'd everyone the day we headed here. Gina said that going with the crowd was a guaranteed death sentence. She was right. I think that's why there was such a big fire. We think, but we don't know for sure, that someone set fire to the protected area. We think that someone who was bit got through and into the safe zone. It was the mall. I think. They set up a chain link fence around it."

"But there have been zombies. We've just been…" Rachel paused and swallowed hard, "…dealing with them. You know? When we see one, we lure it, then we kill it."

"With what?"

"Field hockey sticks."

Melissa looked down at her chosen weapon. "They are good for that."

Lee nodded. "Where are the bodies? We didn't see—"

"Behind the middle house of the cul-de-sac. We didn't want to…you know…look at them." Heather shook her head. "We've been foraging from house to house in this area. It's been good but we're a little worried. It's getting cold. We think the pipes might freeze. We don't have a lot of stored water."

"Come with us back to the school." Joe looked around. "There's plenty of room and we have a well. So no water concerns."

Nicholas shifted to put a protective arm around Rachel. "But what about Jeff? I thought you didn't want to go back."

Joe glanced at Heather. "Things have changed."

Lee lifted his chin. "We'll deal with Jeff when we get back. Whether or not his threat was real there will be a reckoning. We'll announce what he did at the first assembly."

Heather and Rachel looked at each other. "Jeff who and what'd he do?"

"Meadows. Mr. Eagle Scout said that he wouldn't let us back into the academy walls unless we got at least all of the staples on the foraging lists." Lee dug into his backpack next to his chair and came up with the list. "Stuff to get us all through the winter. He's pretty damn sure that if we don't those at the academy will starve."

"How many of you are left?" Heather and Rachel exchanged another glance.

"Twenty-six. Five faculty. Twenty-one students." Joe shrugged. "And I think he's going to have a fit if we don't come back with all of his staples and more when we bring you two with us."

"Fuck him having a fit." Melissa did not look up but the venom in her voice was clear. "He basically threatened to murder us."

Rachel nodded to Heather and Heather nodded back before taking a breath. "We may have a solution…but it's going to be dangerous. Hold on." Heather got up and retrieved a letter and a map from the kitchen. She spread the map out on the living room table between them. "Okay. Along with the letter, Todd and Sheena left us this map and directions to a prepper's house."

"His house or someone else's?" Lee asked.

"Someone else's. Rory Meredith. He said that Rory was out hunting and he bet the bunker was empty of people but was filled with supplies." Heather consulted the letter. "Supplies, weapons, solar power, and a walled yard. We can get to the bunker through the basement of the house. And if Rory is there, he's the type who is happy to trade for supplies and stuff."

Lee didn't want to ask the question because the map seemed to have the answer but he had to confirm his thoughts. "Where is this apocalyptic paradise?"

"That's the sucky part." Heather leaned over the map and pointed. "We're here. The bunker is here."

The two locations couldn't have been farther apart without being in another city. It was a good seven miles as the crow flies but that included walking right by the hospital, the mall, and three churches. If they went through the outside edge of the valley it was at least ten. "It'll take two, maybe three, days to get there. One if it weren't for zombies." Lee pointed to the east edge of the valley.

Joe leaned forward. "We could do it. Move steady and quiet. Is this bunker worth it?"

Heather shrugged. "I don't know for sure. But, yeah. I think so. The way Gina talked, the preppers in the area were well stocked. This could be a really good place to hunker down for the winter."

Lee shook his head. "We need to get supplies back to the academy. But if this is a good place we can use it as a main staging place for future runs."

"Or…we could get people who aren't assholes and bring them back to the bunker." Melissa's voice still had a hard edge to it. "We do what we promised but nothing says we have to stay at the academy. I'm not sure I want to after what Jeff's done."

Nicholas nodded. "I get you but let's not count our bunkers before they're cracked.

"Right." Lee stood. "We move out in the morning. Heather, Rachel, you don't have to come with us—" A clamor of disagreement erupted on all sides of him. Lee held up his hands to calm everyone. "I'm just giving them the choice. This *is* dangerous."

Rachel and Heather exchanged another glance and nodded to each other. "No. We're coming. We trust you guys. And really, we never thought we'd see another living soul again. We're not giving that up."

"All right. Then we move out in the morning. We'll spend the rest of the day prepping you two and figuring out our exact plans. Joe, Nick? You help them and teach them our hand signals?"

"Can do." Joe nodded. "Will do."

* * *

The Harridan was the last person Michael expected to have knocking on his door in the late afternoon. More surprising was the fact that she had a half full bottle of whiskey with her. This gift of the gods appeared out of her bag as soon as she sat down on his couch. "I bring an olive branch."

Michael wasn't one to look a gift horse—or gift alcohol—in the mouth. He came up with two lowball glasses and set them on the table as she opened the bottle. "What brought this on?"

Kimberly poured him a glass until he smiled. Then she poured her own. She watched him take a healthy swallow and savor the taste. "We both know one of us will need to do the work of running what's left of the Salton Academy now that Swenson killed himself. It can be you with me helping or me with you helping or not. Either way, I come with a proposal. First…which would rather: you leading or me?"

Michael rubbed his lips, looking at the woman, still surprised at her bluntness. "It depends on the proposal," he hedged, giving himself time to think. Being in charge would be great but it would mean work, not something he was inclined to do if he could get away with it. Not being in charge meant he could have to listen to her, but then he wouldn't have to do much of anything he didn't want to. He took another long swallow of the whiskey. It burned so good all the way down.

"The proposal is separate. I'd rather settle the leadership problem." Kimberly wet her lips with her whiskey but didn't drink.

He realized that she was nervous. Swenson offing himself upset her. Michael considered prolonging her nervousness but the whiskey was already getting to him. The pleasant tingling in his arms told him it had been too long since he had had a real drink. "Really, you should lead but only if you'll listen to the rest of the faculty as your council. Too much work for me but I do have good ideas."

She sat back and nodded, relaxing, watching him. "All right. I can do that. You can still run Hadfield?"

"Of course." Michael took a smaller swallow to pace himself. "Now, this proposal?"

Kimberly leaned forward and refilled his glass. Then, she took a breath. "I want you to leave the girls alone. All of them. In exchange…you can have me."

The anger that had started to boil up stopped. "Have…you?" Michael picked up his glass to cover his confusion. He took another gulp of whiskey. "What do you mean?"

She put her glass down and looked him in the eye. "Have me any way you want—sexually. You want me sweet and begging? I can do that. You want me sassy and fighting you? I can do that. But I'll surrender to you. You want to tie me up? I'm down. You want me to tie you up? I can do that, too. Blow job, anal beads, pearl necklace? I'm yours anywhere and when as long as you leave the rest alone." Kimberly smiled as Michael's eyes got wider and wider.

His mouth had gone dry as she spoke words he never even dreamt she would say. "Starting when?" Michael still couldn't believe it. He stared at the handsome woman, realizing that everything she said struck a nerve.

"Now." She stood up and took her jacket off. Still standing, she slowly unbuttoned her shirt until she stood there with her shirt open and lacy white bra showing against her ebon skin. "Do we have a deal?"

"Deal?" Michael threw back the last of his whiskey and carefully put the empty glass on the table. "Hell, yeah. Why do I want a girl when I could have a woman?" He knew he lied in every word but she didn't have to know that until it was too late. He stood and wavered, suddenly dizzy. "Too much booze." He sat back down. "C'mere, girl. You said something about a blow job…"

Kimberly pulled the low table out of the way then went down to her hands and knees. She sensuously crawled over to him. As she crawled, she dipped her hand into her purse and grabbed the syringe full of morphine. He lolled his head back as she reached his knees. "You just relax. Let me take care of you."

Michael mumbled something incoherent and waved a hand at her as she ran a hand up his thigh. Then, he didn't respond at all.

Kimberly stood and moved around to the side of the chair as Michael began to snore big open-mouthed snores. She shoved his head to the side, found the artery in his neck and pushed the needle in like Nancy showed her. Michael barely reacted. It was just too bad she had had to waste half a bottle of good whiskey to do this, Kimberly thought as she depressed the plunger all the way in.

Sudden shouting in the hallway brought her head up and her heart to her throat.

CHAPTER
NINE

T hink Evan's getting some from Athena?" Aaron snickered at the thought as the three boys headed to the gym for some basketball.

Shane shrugged. "Don't know. Haven't seen him." He paused, stuffing his hands in his jean pockets—long gone were the days of academy uniforms—and smirked. "If he is, more power to him. He should get something to hold onto for a bit."

"If he is, she'd better be careful with him. She'll break him otherwise." Aaron grinned the stopped in at the gym door to pantomime having sex, then breaking his back. Shane laughed. Ross didn't.

"Don't be like that." Ross pushed past the other two and opened the gym door. "Evan's a good guy. Just because his dad was a douche doesn't mean he has to suffer too." Ross sped up as Aaron followed close behind. "Shit, I hope he's balls deep in Athena. He deserves something good."

Shane lagged back as Aaron and Ross suddenly sprinted, racing each other to the door to the back hallway where the equipment was kept. Not in the equipment cage anymore but in the side hallway lockers. Even with the apocalypse Swenson and Shin had insisted that the gymnasium rules had to be kept and the equipment had to be put away. Shane looked around. "Guys, do you smell something funny?"

Aaron paused as Ross reached for the door. "What? Like that damn dog?"

Ross opened the hallway door and hell came tumbling out in the form of grasping hands, scrabbling claws, and snapping teeth. Athena and Evan grabbed Ross as he yelled, flailing at them. Beauregard leapt for Aaron who put his arm up as a shield against those lethal jaws. Just as the dog bit down on his jacket-covered forearm, Aaron swung himself around, throwing the dog into Athena, causing the entire struggling group to go down.

Shane looked around. He saw no weapons he could use to help anyone. Ross screamed a wordless sound of agony as Evan and Athena both ripped into his flesh. Aaron scrambled backwards as Beauregard was distracted by vulnerable, trapped flesh.

"Run!" Shane, already following his own advice, sprinted back to the gym door.

"Go! Go! Go!" Aaron ran as fast as his stout legs would carry him, not looking to see if the dog was chasing him or not.

They both got out of the before Ross quit screaming in pain. "Holy fuck. Holy fuck! Holy fuck!" Aaron grabbed chain that used to lock the gym at night and wrapped it around the door handles.

"Did it get you? Are you bit?" Shane stood back from Aaron, looking like he was ready to run from his friend.

Aaron looked at his leather jacket sleeve. There were tears but no blood. He shook his head. "No. It didn't get through my jacket." He looked up at the sky. "Thank you, Mom!"

"C'mon. We gotta tell everyone. Fuck. Evan...Athena. Ross..."

"I know. I know."

The two boys sprinted across the quad. All the while Aaron tried not to think about the fact that he caused his friend's death. Ross might have gotten away if he hadn't knocked them all over. The pain of Aaron's guilt, and the adrenaline coursing through his system, masked the small pain where a single canine tooth broke the skin on his arm in a small scratch less than an inch long.

"Zombies!" Shane yelled as he burst through the front door of Hadfield Hall. "Zombies in the gymnasium! Zombies!" As he yelled, the boys who could hear him scrambled for weapons. Some came tumbling down the stairs. Others immediately hid.

Aaron didn't bother to yell. He ran up the stairs to his room to get his baseball bat. He wondered how in the hell he could've ever stopped carrying at least one weapon at all times.

* * *

Kimberly listened to the shouts in the hallway. The only word she could make out was *zombie* and it was a bad word to hear any time of day or night. She pulled the syringe from Michael's neck and hid it in her purse. A firm touch to his neck looking for a pulse told her that the first syringe had done its job. Michael was dead and she didn't need to use the second syringe. That was a relief.

After a moment's pause she locked Michael's door. She didn't want the students to see her in here. She took her glass and the whiskey bottle to the kitchenette. As she dumped the rest of the whiskey out with one hand, she emptied her full glass with the other. She could hear kids running above her. Putting the glass to the side, she returned to the living room and pushed the low table back in front of Michael.

While she moved with smooth efficiency, inside she was screaming in terror. Zombies. Inside the walls. It was a terror she stomped on as she arranged the empty whiskey bottle, the empty glass, and the empty Percocet bottle on its side with the cap tossed artfully next to it. Kimberly stood back as she buttoned up her blouse, surveying the scene. Unable to deal with the mantle of responsibility Professor Michael Leeds decided to take the coward's way out…just like the principal had.

After putting on her jacket and picking up her purse, Kimberly crept to the door and listened. The expected pounding on the door came. "Professor Leeds! Professor Leeds!" She couldn't tell which panicked boy was calling for the dead man. The pounding came again. "Professor Leeds! There's zombies in the gymnasium!"

Suddenly Kimberly could see what had happened to Evan, and maybe Athena. Evan had gone to see his dog…and the dog escaped, turning him. She bowed her head. She knew she should've insisted on that dog being killed but she felt so sorry for Evan. Shaking her head Kimberly knew her sympathy was at fault. She had been too soft.

"You! Go to Swenson's office. Leeds might be there. You! Go to Bonny Hall. Tell Mrs. Hood. You, go to the Nurse, let her know." Kimberly recognized this voice. Jeff. Mr. Eagle Scout himself. Bless the kid who had sense enough to keep his head in a crisis. "Get everyone inside and to shelter in place. Bonny

Hall. We'll meet at Bonny Hall common room. I'm going to see if I can find Shin. Weapons, everyone!"

She listened to running feet and waited until there was silence. Slowly opening the door, Kimberly peeked out. The hallway was empty. She slipped out of Michael's suite and closed it behind her, making sure to close it all the way, engaging the latch and the lock. She tried the doorknob. It wouldn't budge.

Just as Kimberly was about to leave, she heard running feet on the stairs. She didn't want to be caught loitering here. Instead, she knocked firmly on Michael's door. "Michael. Michael! It's is an emergency!" She struggled with the locked doorknob. She turned and hurried to Shin's room and knocked there. "Shin! Are you there? Shin!" She tried his doorknob and wasn't surprised to find it locked. "Damnit." Kimberly allowed herself to feel some of the pent up panic.

"We can't find them."

Kimberly looked up. Ron. One of Jeff's friends. She hurried towards him. "Shin must be on perimeter patrol. I don't know where Professor Leeds is. He's not answering his door."

Ron shook his head, looking scared. He held a crowbar in a white-knuckled grip. "You gotta come upstairs. It's Shane."

She felt the blood drain from her face. "What happened? Did he get bit? Is he okay?"

Ron shook his head. "I don't know." Then he took off running up the stairs.

Kimberly didn't say anything, tried not to think of anything, but knew if a student was alive but had been bitten they *would* have to be put down for the good of all. It was a worst case scenario.

Ron led her up to the third floor and stopped before a closed door. He pointed at it. "In there."

Kimberly nodded and squared her shoulders, preparing herself for everything except for what happened next. She opened the door and stepped into the room. Jeff looked up from his preparations—he was buckling on a homemade weapon holster over a heavy jacket. "Mrs. Hood?"

"Where's Shane? What's—" Kimberly's words were cut off as Ron hit her as hard as he could in the back of the head. She crumpled to the ground without a word, part of her head caved in.

"Jesus mother pussbucket!" Jeff jumped back.

"Nope. But close." Ron grinned. "Let's get her somewhere and finish her off. No time like the present with everyone panicking."

"What the hell?" Jeff gave him a long, considering look. This wasn't what he had planned.

"What? She was on the list." Ron looked put out. "She was right there. Everyone else is gone like you told them to be. It was too good to pass up." When Jeff still didn't say anything, Ron shifted, his voice persuasive. "Look, one less mouth to feed. I think that's all we needed anyway if what Shane and Aaron said were true."

This snapped Jeff out of his stunned judgment of Ron's sanity. He nodded. "You're right and she was on the list. Right after Leeds. And I think we can manage him so he doesn't have to die, too." Jeff looked down at Mrs. Hood's unmoving body to avoid looking at Ron's satisfied leer. Right now they had to get the body out of his room before it leaked all over the place. "4th floor? No one is using any of those rooms."

Ron nodded and helped put the dorm mistress's unresisting body over Jeff's shoulder. "Didn't even get much blood on your floor either. But, hold on." Ron took the bottle of cough syrup off Jeff's desk, spilled it on the floor, then threw a towel on top of the mess, before putting the open container back on the desk.

Jeff shrugged. It was a good enough cover for now. "Spot for me."

Ron nodded and grabbed Mrs. Hood's dropped purse before he made sure there was no one in the hallway.

Ron and Jeff hurried up to the fourth floor and chose one of the rooms at random. Jeff dropped her to the floor. "How do you want to do it?"

"Strangle her?" Ron suggested.

Jeff shook his head. "Too likely to wake up. Slit her throat. Or rather, just cut one of the arteries. Make it look like she came up here to suicide."

"I like it." Ron grinned. "Make it look like she was hiding and couldn't hack it." He manhandled her body into the closet and she moaned but didn't wake up. Ron pulled his buck knife from his pocket, flipped it open, and offered it handle first to Jeff. "Want the honors?"

Jeff shook his head. "Nah. You go ahead."

Ron gave him a long look then shrugged. He grabbed her left wrist and sliced her deep up the arm. "Down, not across," he murmured, his eyes far away. He licked his lips as he watched the blood well up and spill over.

Kimberly's eyes fluttered open as he cut her right wrist in a single long slash. "Wha…?"

"Shh. You've had an accident, Mrs. Hood. Don't move. Stay put." Ron's voice was soft and caring. Her eyes rolled in her head and she slumped forward again. "Good girl. It'll be okay." He cleaned the knife off on her jacket.

Jeff looked down at Mrs. Hood's purse, feeling sick to his stomach. But what he saw, pushed that to the side. He hunkered over her purse and opened. "Whoa. What's this?" He pulled out an empty syringe, a full syringe, and a full bottle of morphine. "Well, looks like the Harridan was a drug addict. Interesting." He put the empty syringe back in the purse and considered the morphine for a long time.

"Playtime for another day." Ron stepped back from the growing puddle of blood. "Blood flow's slowing. She's dead soon."

"You head to Bonny. Tell everyone I'm checking the Commons and I'll be there soon with some food. We need to make a plan to deal with the zombies." Jeff stood and moved the purse into the closet. He put the full syringe and morphine in a pocket. "If we're lucky, the zombies are only in the gym. But we can't count on it."

"You want me to watch your back?" Ron closed the closet door.

Jeff shook his head. "No. Get control of Bonny. Help Krenshaw and Leeds if you have to. We need to get every living person in one place for a headcount. I need to know how many zombies we have to kill. We're not leaving a single one of them alive this time."

CHAPTER
TEN

Nancy closed her eyes in a brief prayer after Ken—quiet, dependable Ken—burst into the infirmary and told her what had happened to Evan, Athena, and Ross. Lord knows how the dog got free but it was clear what happened next. Even as these thoughts flitted through her mind she was packing the last of her necessary infirmary gear into her medical bag. "Did anyone else get bit?"

"No, ma'am. Not that I know of. It was a close call for Aaron, I heard." Ken shifted from foot to foot, keeping his dark, almond shaped eyes on Nurse Krenshaw. "That's why Jeff said we should all get to Bonny Hall and shelter in place. Get a headcount and all."

"What did Mrs. Hood say?"

"I don't know. I haven't seen her. I came straight here."

"All right. Let's get going. Carry that bag for me and keep your weapon handy." Nancy held her own weapon, a guard baton that she had gotten from Shin, at the ready.

"Yes, ma'am."

* * *

The Bonny Hall common room boiled over with excited, fearful chatter as the boys, ordered to come, milled about with the girls, talking with Shane and Aaron about what had happened in the gymnasium. It all stopped when Nurse Krenshaw came in with Ken. She took one look at the group and nodded.

"Sophia, Rose. Take these to the makeshift infirmary." Nancy's voice was quavery but confident as she gestured to the bags she and Ken were holding. "Then come back here. Make it quick." She looked around the room. "The rest of you, have a seat."

Nancy waited until the girls had returned and everyone had settled. "All right. Who are we missing?" She waved her hands for quiet as voices started calling out names. "I need a roll sheet."

Pria raised her hand. "I have a list. It's not complete." She held out a notebook.

"Read out the girl's names."

"Toni. Rose. Sophia. Maya." As she read each name, the girl raised her hand to be counted. "Pria." Pria raised her own hand. "Melissa is out. And Athena…they said…she was in the gym."

Nancy nodded. "Shane or Aaron? Is that true?"

Shane nodded, rubbing the side of his mouth. "Evan and Athena were there. They got Ross."

The old woman sighed. "All right. The boys?" she prompted Pria.

"John. Ken. Aaron. Shane. Ron. Caleb. Jeff." She paused when she got to Jeff's name and there was no raised hand.

"He's at the Commons, getting us food. He'll be here soon." Ron shifted in his seat. "He said we should get a headcount to see who is missing and if there are more zombies than in the gym."

"Very good." Nancy gestured to Pria again.

The Indian girl looked at her list. "I know Nick, Lee, and Joe are out. Evan and Ross...are dead. But I'm missing someone."

"Me." Steve raised his hand. "Steve."

"Right." Pria wrote on her notepad.

Nancy frowned. "Deceased we know are: Principal Swenson, Evan, Ross, and Athena." She looked around. "Where are Mrs. Hood, Professor Leeds, and Shin?"

"Shin is probably patrolling. But he should be back by dark." This was Caleb. "But I don't know about the other two."

"In that case, we should have someone watching for Shin. We need to intercept him before he goes to patrol the gym."

"We put a chain around the gym doors but we couldn't find the lock for it." Aaron rubbed at his forearm.

She nodded to him. The opening of the dorm's front door stopped what Nancy was going to say next. Jeff entered with a full backpack and Shin following behind with a case of water. The two of them stopped in the entry way and stared at the mass of people looking at them. Nancy noted that several of the students had grabbed their weapons in response to the sudden noise.

Jeff looked at them, clipped his bat to his belt holster, and shifted the backpack to the floor. "I brought dinner."

That broke the growing tension in the room as the ever-hungry kids jumped up to receive whatever dinner was. In this case, it was crackers, a variety of canned meat, canned cheese spread, and bottled water. It was a chaos of distributing the food with paper towels and making sure that everyone got something to eat. As things went, it would be a light meal. But until the threat assessment could be made it was the best Jeff could do.

Once everyone was eating Nancy beckoned Shin to her. Jeff followed. When she gave him a look he pretended obviousness. "What did we miss?"

Nancy frowned for a moment then shrugged. "We have accounting of everyone except for Professor Leeds and Mrs. Hood. There are four zombies in the gymnasium—three students and one dog—and we don't know what happened to the faculty members."

"We should post guards tonight. To make sure there are no breaches to security." Shin kept his voice low and quiet. He turned to Jeff. "Do you think that is something you can organize? Two students a shift, two or three shifts? Interior patrols and 4th floor lookouts?"

Jeff nodded. "Absolutely. Also, maybe we should organize a quick run to Hadfield for the boys to get stuff they left behind?" He looked at the frown on the Nurse's face. "Tomorrow. When it's light and we can see."

Shin and Nancy looked at each other. Shin nodded. Then Nancy nodded. "All right. But tonight the boys sleep on the first floor in their clothes. And no wandering. Tell that to your patrols."

Jeff nodded and bowed his head for a moment. "Okay. Anything else?" He glanced up at them.

"Thank you for bringing us dinner." Nancy smiled a distracted, worried smile. "That was kind of you."

"It's my job. I'm the cook." Jeff turned and made his way to his knot of close friends. He pulled a can of tuna out of his bag as he sat down.

* * *

For a long moment, the two adults watched the students sit around the common room, eat, joke, and laugh. Aaron's voice rose as he insisted that mixing spam and tuna on a cracker was good. He bit half of one cracker and made exaggerated noises of pleasure. Toni grinned, accepted the second half, ate it, and looked surprised. Ken, John, Shane, and Rose all laughed and made up their own meat, cheese, and cracker concoctions to share. Pria and Maya sat to the side with their heads together, talking quietly over their food.

Shin turned to Nancy. "You needed something else?"

"I'm so glad you're back. Where've you been?" Nancy drew him away from the common room and away from where prying ears could overhear.

"Michael sent me to do a more thorough search of the woods for the missing students. It was a sound enough request. I was just coming back to report when Jeff came out of the boys' dorm with a backpack and his baseball bat. I knew something was wrong when he hailed me. He told me what had happened, that they couldn't find Michael, and asked me to help him bring food and to watch his back. I could not refuse."

Nancy's lips pressed into a line of concern before she spoke. "We have a problem."

"Michael and Kimberly?"

She nodded. "Kimberly went to confront Michael about sleeping with Sophia and threatening her when she cut it off. You saw what he did at the assembly."

Shin was quiet, thinking. "I see. Do you believe Michael could've hurt Kimberly?"

Nancy hesitated, not willing to tell him the truth. "Maybe. I don't know."

"Perhaps he heard the word 'zombie' and decided to remain hidden in his suite."

"Maybe. I don't know. I know it's getting dark and we don't know if there are more zombies inside the walls…but would you check?"

"Of course. Also, I should get a lock on that chain to keep the zombies in the gymnasium until we can safely exterminate them." Shin zipped up his jacket. "I'll do that now."

Toni nudged Rose as Shin's departure caught most of the students' attention. "My room, midnight. You, me, Shane, Aaron, and a bottle of the good stuff."

Rose's eyes widened and she grinned. "You got some left?"

"A whole bottle of rum. Unopened." Toni nodded. "It's as good of a time as any. Tell Shane and bring your mattress."

"You bet."

The two of them giggled in anticipation of the private party.

* * *

Shin did not use his flashlight as he moved through the twilight of the evening. He kept his baton out and his senses alert for anything unusual and any unidentifiable sound. The only thing he felt was a distinct drop in the temperature. Winter was closing in fast. Again he wondered how the students on the supply run were doing. He hoped they were well and would be back soon.

He entered Hadfield Hall and went directly to Michael's door on quiet feet. He stood outside the door for a count of sixty, listening for any movement within the suite. After hearing nothing he knocked politely and listened for a count of thirty. "Professor Leeds, it's Shin. I'm reporting in." He knocked a second time. Then he pulled his ring of master keys from his pocket, found the right key, and opened the suite door.

The room was dark but there was still enough ambient light to see the silhouette of the man sitting in the chair with his head slumped. "Professor Leeds? Michael?" Shin frowned and pulled out his small flashlight. Light sparkled in the glass of the empty whiskey bottle and lowball glass as he shone it on the professor. Shin's frown deepened as he moved into the room, closing the door behind him.

He took a close look at the alcohol bottle, then picked up the empty bottle of Percocet. Shin's frown became a scowl. "Suicide. A real one this time. Coward." He moved to the body and felt for a pulse at the wrist and neck. Shin wasn't surprised when he didn't find one. "What did you do with Kimberly? Hmmm?"

Two things could have happened. Kimberly confronted Michael, who then killed her and committed suicide or Kimberly confronted Michael, left, and then he committed suicide. But where was the dorm mistress? Shin moved through the suite, opening room and closet doors. Kimberly wasn't to be found.

He took the time to do a quick patrol of the entire building, opening every room looking for sign of her, even checking the attic but Kimberly was nowhere around. Then he thought about the gymnasium and shook his head. He prayed she hadn't gone in there try to do…what? Kill the zombies? Rescue the unreachable? Once bitten the infected was dead and it was up to everyone else to deal with it as quickly and efficiently as possible.

Shin let out a sigh. Either way he wouldn't be able to find out tonight. He had to get a lock on the building and figure out how to look inside to see who all was in there. The lock would be tonight. The rest would have to wait until tomorrow.

* * *

The four of them were curled up on mattresses on Toni's floor. Toni and Aaron were on one mattress. Shane and Rose were on the other one. They all cuddled under comforters in varying states of undress that would become total before the night was through. Who was going to sleep with whom would start with the couples as is. But by the morning it was anyone's guess. It wasn't the first time they would experiment with their sexuality but it would be the last.

"I had to promise Jeff that the four of us would stand watch tomorrow. Otherwise two of us were going to have to do it tonight. He didn't care that we had plans." Shane shrugged.

"Who died and made him God?" Toni asked as she passed the bottle of spiced rum to Aaron.

Aaron raised the bottle in a mock toast. "Swenson did. And face it, the guy knows his shit. If he wants to do all the work, I say let him." He took a deep swallow from the bottle before passing it to Rose.

"Yeah. Whatever." Toni shook her head. "He's such a know-it-all." She took the bottle from Rose and drank. "I don't like him."

Rose took the bottle back. "Don't worry about it, hon. He's out there walking a patrol while we're in here getting drunk." Rose handed the bottle to Shane.

"Sucks to be him right now." Shane took the bottle and a kiss from Rose.

Aaron rubbed his arm. The muscles were sore. "Fucking dog."

"You okay?" Toni looked at his arm.

"Yeah. It was just a heavy dog." Aaron shrugged. "Not every day I have to throw a sixty pound mutt off me." He and Shane exchanged a look that said neither of them would ever tell he threw the dog into the rest, making it impossible for Ross to escape.

Toni kissed his arm. "Does that make it feel better?"

"C'mere. I'll show you what'll make me feel a lot better." He grabbed her in a bear hug and pulled her giggling to the mattress.

Rose and Shane turned from them and focused on each other.

* * *

Outside, the first snow of the year began to fall.

PLAN
FOR THE
FUTURE

ELEVEN

Lee's face was grey with fear as he climbed down from the water tower. He looked at his five companions. None of them said anything at his expression but he saw that they suddenly mirrored his fear. Lee swallowed. He knew he needed to keep it together. "Well, there's good news and there's bad news…and there's worse news."

"Lay it on us." Nicholas pulled Rachel to him to comfort and receive comfort. The rest nodded.

Melissa moved to Lee's side as he spoke. "Good news: I think I see our target. It's got actual stone walls all the way around the place and I didn't see any zombies within them. We'll be there in the next hour or so. Bad news: There's zombies between us and it. We might be able to sneak by. Worse news: I think half of the city is clustered around the mall. There is no way we can get into it or the hospital. It would be suicide."

Melissa glanced up at to the top of the water tower. "I thought we might've had a chance to save Evan."

Lee shook his head, his voice sad. "No. We wouldn't make it. I wish…"

Joe furrowed his brow, keeping his voice low. "But our current target isn't impossible?"

"No. It's not. We've been lucky, moving slow and steady. Most of the zombies died in the city center and not on the edges. The ones we've dealt with were people who'd been bitten, probably hidden it, then died out here." Lee glanced up at the water tower before meeting Joe's eyes. "This last bit is going to be bad."

"How bad?" Heather raised her chin, gripping her hockey stick tight.

"There's at least a dozen zombies on the edges we need to pass through. That I could see." Lee looked to each member of his little band. "If we can't sneak past them, we'd have to kill every single one that sees us without alerting any of the others."

Nicholas pulled out the map and looked at it. "What about traveling through the creek?" He pointed to the creek on the map. "I know it's cold but…"

Lee shook his head. "No. Too slippery. Too hemmed in. Too easy to be ambushed. I couldn't see who or what was down there because of the tree cover. We're going to have to go from yard to yard." He looked around the group again. "Are we ready?" When no one dissented he stood straight. "Right. Scout, over the wall, sneak through. Scout. If we see an easier way to get into a yard we take it."

The plan worked for the first three yards.

* * *

Joe took point on the fourth yard. There was no easy way in. The six foot wooden fence felt sturdy enough but it had the look of age to it—unpainted, sun bleached, and split boards. The wood creaked as he clambered over and landed on the other side. Everyone waited and held their collective breath for the signal that all was well.

"C'mon." The word was whispered through two of the boards.

Nicholas laced his fingers together to give Lee a boost over. Lee pushed off and transferred his weight to his hands on the top of the fence, his momentum carrying him over. That's what should have happened. Instead, at the apex of Lee's leap as he pushed down, the dilapidated fence cracked in half and collapsed to the ground with Lee on top of it. The crashing of the broken fence was tremendous in the silence of the dead world.

No one moved as Lee stayed where he was on the ground, the tang of blood suddenly scenting the air. The sound of rising moans from the other side of the houses spurred the group to action. Joe grabbed Lee, pulling him to his feet. The rest could see him gritting his teeth to keep from crying out at the foot long shard of wood, as thick as a man's finger, piercing his shoulder.

"The house!" Melissa's voice was a harsh whisper. Everyone obeyed. No one wanted to be out in the open around fresh blood after the cacophony they'd just made. With the section of fence gone, it was only a matter of scrabbling over splintered wood to get into the yard.

Heather was the first to the door. She found it unlocked and opened it, keeping her hockey stick in front of her. Joe followed half carrying Lee. Melissa, Rachel, and Nicholas wasted no time getting inside the house and locking the door.

The stench of rotten vegetables and meat greeted them as they huddled inside. Joe signaled for Rachel and Nicholas to keep watch as he pulled Lee deeper into the house. Heather and Melissa bracketed them, keeping their weapons at the ready.

Lee gritted his teeth together in an effort to keep from screaming as every movement ground wood into flesh. He panted through clenched teeth as Joe lowered him into a kitchen chair. Keeping his voice to a low mumble that would not carry, Joe said, "Heather, you, me, clear the house and get a first aid kit. Melissa, keep him quiet."

With a nod Melissa took Joe's place at Lee's side as the other two left the room. "Shh…" she murmured, holding his uninjured hand. "It'll be out soon."

Lee slowed his panting breaths as he looked over at the piece of wood sticking out of his shoulder. "Sugar water. Keep energy up in blood loss."

Even though the words were barely audible Melissa understood and reacted. She left her hockey stick on the kitchen table and began rummaging through the cabinets looking for what she needed as Lee watched. Neither of them saw the pantry door slowly swing open.

*　*　*

The zombie lunged and latched onto Lee's injured arm, ripping the flesh with savage teeth. Lee couldn't stop the cry of pain and alarm that erupted from his mouth as the dead child yanked his injured arm towards it. Melissa dropped the bag of sugar, whirling in surprised panic. Her shout of "No!" mingled with Lee's continuing yells as he punched at the zombie kid's head.

Melissa grabbed her hockey stick and brought down on the zombie's head with a sharp crack. Even as the zombie let go of Lee's arm, stumbling back, Melissa advanced, beating the zombie as hard as she could. Every strike was punctuated with her sobbing, "No! No!" She didn't stop pummeling the zombie when it fell and the gore splattered about the kitchen. She didn't stop when Joe and Heather returned in alarm. Nor did she stop when Joe gave warning, "The blood!" and pulled Heather from the kitchen.

It took Lee grabbing her by the arm to halt her crazed denial of what had just happened. "It's done, Mel. It's dead." His soft voice took on a note of alarm. "Melissa, your face."

Melissa touched her face. It was covered in the dead zombie's blood. "Oh God."

Joe and Heather peeked back in. "We've got to move to the basement. I've cleared it. Now." The strained looks on their faces and the louder sounds of moaning outside the house spurred Lee and Melissa into action and the six survivors hurried to the relative safety of the basement.

The basement, fully underground with no windows, had been stocked with emergency gear along with boxes and unused exercise equipment. In short order Heather had Melissa to the side and had cleaned all of the gore off her face with wet wipes while Nicholas and Joe tended to Lee, getting the wood out of his shoulder and bandaging up both it and the bite wound.

Lee grabbed Joe's arm before he could move off. "We've got to stay here for at least a day." He continued at Joe unasked question. "If was just me I'd deal with myself and have you make sure I was dead. But Melissa…she might be infected, she might not. We don't know for sure. We've got to know before you continue on."

Denial and resignation warred on Joe's face. "Well, we can't leave until the rabble calms down anyway. And there's food and some supplies here."

"We should manifest symptoms at the same time. If she's infected, we were infected at the same time." Lee didn't let go of Joe's arm. He pulled his friend closer. "If she's infected I'll do it. If she's not you've got to make sure she goes with you. And don't let her see me. You know the rule: We don't leave injured behind. Only dead."

Joe wanted to deny Lee but his wrapped arm refused them a happy ending. He put a hand over Lee's. "Promise."

* * *

Pria and Maya slept back to back in twin-sized bed with Maya closest to the wall. Pria knew what the rest would say if they saw this. Lewd jokes and offers for a threesome probably. She didn't care. Things were falling apart. "I think we should consider separating ourselves from the rest. Just to be sure. Father said that crowds were dangerous. Now we're all crowded in here."

"No." Maya put a hand on the wall, feeling how cold it had gotten. "Not yet. We've got our plan, sis, but we don't need to enact it yet. The zombies are only in the gym."

"Things are breaking. People are breaking."

"We won't break."

Pria's voice softened. "I'm afraid others might break and hurt us. I promised Father…"

Maya turned over so she was spooning with her sister. "I know. But now is not the time to run. It's gotten cold. The fourth floor will be freezing. Literally. We didn't think about the heat except to get blankets. We should focus on that. Plus, we can't hide now without everyone figuring out where we've gone. Not when the toilet flushes and sounds throughout the building."

As if to prove her point the sound of rushing water below them, though muffled, told them that someone on the first or second floor had just flushed a toilet.

"All right. I don't like it but you're right about the heat. But we don't separate unless we have to."

"Agreed." Maya hugged Pria tight. "We'll be okay. The zombies are trapped. Shin and the rest will deal with them. Then things will go back to normal. All we'll really have to worry about is keeping the rest from knowing about our shelter and from turning on us if they do."

Pria patted Maya's hand. "They won't. You're right. We'll be okay. I'll make sure of it."

"We'll both make sure of it." Maya turned back over and scooted closer to the wall to make sure she didn't accidently push Pria out of bed in the middle of the night.

* * *

Aaron rolled over and moaned softly. He had the absolute worst headache ever. His rising gorge made him sit up, then make a run for the bathroom in his skivvies. He made it in time to vomit up what was left of his dinner and what had been consumed at the mini-party he'd had with Toni, Rose, and Shane. "A hangover? Really? Damn, I'm a fucking lightweight these days."

He rinsed his mouth out and sighed, feeling how sore his neck was as he stretched it. As he gulped water from the tap and splashed it over his head he wondered if it really was a hangover or if he'd caught something. The flu. He remembered how bad that was. "Sucks to be all of us," he muttered to the mirror. If he was actually sick it was a good bet his friends were too after last night.

Shuffling back to Toni's room he gave a mental shrug. It really didn't surprise him. Between the principal's suicide, the zombies in the gym, and the general stress of living in an apocalyptic world, he wondered how it'd been so long since any of the students had gotten really sick.

He snuggled close to Toni, vaguely aware of the heat coming off both of them. Yep. Sick. It wasn't so bad in the chill of the room. It'd gotten really cold.

*　*　*

"What do you think is going to happen to us when the supply team gets back?" Steve pulled his coat closed as the sound of the wind outside was amplified in the front stairwell.

"What do you mean?" Ron paused on the steps and cocked his head to one side, studying Steve. It was just after one in the morning. The two of them were about halfway through the second hour of their six hour watch. They'd just about finished the second walkthrough of their patrol.

"I mean they aren't going to just let go of what Jeff said about them not getting back in the walls."

Ron lowered his voice. "Are we really going to have this conversation?"

Normally Steve backed down at the dangerous look in Ron's eyes but this time he didn't. It was too serious to let go. Even if it meant that Ron would be mad at him for a while. "We need to have it."

For a moment Ron didn't say anything. Then he nodded. "All right. But not here. Thin walls and big ears. Let's go to the chapel." He didn't wait for a response. He descended to the landing, paused at the door, waiting for Steve to follow, then opened it for the two of them to exit. The two of them moved with quiet speed and Ron made sure to close the door with equal silence.

"It's snowing." Steve zipped his jacket closed. "Came early this year."

"It's not sticking to the sidewalk yet. This might be a fluke." Ron led the way to the chapel and opened the door for them. He glanced around after Steve entered, looking for signs of life. Everything was still and quiet. He entered to find Steve in the antechamber. "What's up?"

"We sure this place is clean?" The slight trembling in Steve's voice betrayed his nervousness.

Ron shrugged. "We only know about the zombies in the gym and Shin has that place locked up."

"What about Mrs. Hood and Professor Leeds?"

"I wouldn't worry about them. Probably fucking somewhere."

Steve couldn't help his grin. "But they hate each other."

"How else are they going to figure out who's going to be on top?" Ron leered, remembering the sound of the crowbar hitting Mrs. Hood's head as he gripped his chosen weapon tighter. He had no idea where Leeds was and, right now, he didn't care. "Okay. What's the deal with *when the supply team gets back*?"

The two of them walked to the back of the chapel where the private apartments of Father Macgregor and Brother Fuller, the two religious leaders on campus, were. Father Macgregor had locked his apartment and no one had been brave enough to risk the faculty's wrath by breaking into it. Ron gave the locked door a speculative thought before he ducked into the apartment that Brother Fuller used to live in during the school year.

It was a simple but comfortable room with a desk, sitting area, bedroom sectioned off with a standing bamboo privacy screen. The other door led to the bathroom shared by both clergy men. The room had the chill of an abandoned building that had gone too long without heat or people. Steve sat down on the couch. "I mean, when they get back, they're going to raise a ruckus. We're going to get in trouble along with Jeff."

Ron didn't sit. Instead, he walked around the sitting area to the bookshelf and pretended examined the books on it. "That's not going to happen."

"Why not? We all agreed to it. I can't imagine someone like Joe keeping his mouth shut. Lee, maybe. If he and Jeff managed to have a private conversation before everything blew up. They're probably going to punish us right along with Jeff."

"Punish us how?"

Steve looked over his shoulder. "What do you mean?"

"I mean, how is someone like Leeds or Krenshaw or Shin going to punish us? You think anyone's going to do anything? What we're doing is for the good of the academy." Ron kept his back to the other boy as he plucked a book, *Age of Reason* by Thomas Paine, from the shelf.

Steve turned back around and shook his head. "I don't think it's going to be that easy."

"I don't think you have your heart in the right place. Jeff would never give us up. If there was a fall he'd take it for the rest of us." He stuffed the book in his pocket. "I don't think you believe in Jeff. I know he believes in you." Ron turned, raising the crowbar over his head. "And think I'm going to have to save him from that."

Steve turned and got an arm up to ward off the lethal blow. He yelled in surprise and pain as his arm broke. Moving with manic speed Ron came around the couch as Steve tumbled to the side, holding his arm. "No!"

Ron's next blow hit his intended target and the sound of a melon falling from a second story greeted his ears. Steve fell back, his forehead crumpled in, blood leaking from it. Ron stood over him, panting, exhilarated. This was better than he had imagined. Ron put the crowbar down and crouched next to Steve's unmoving body.

"Yes," Ron murmured, exulted, as he felt Steve's breath on his face. He straddled the smaller boy's body and gently wrapped his hands around Steve's throat. Then he began to squeeze. Steve never opened his eyes—too bad—but his body bucked a couple of times. An automatic response the body had when fighting for its life Ron had once read.

When it was over, Ron remained straddling Steve's dead body for a long time as he savored the sensation of slowly killing someone. Then he got to work, breaking into Macgregor's apartment through the bathroom door and hiding the body in the trunk amongst Macgregor's priestly robes. Later, he'd come back and search the room for valuables and interesting items.

* * *

In the coldest part of the night, when everyone was sleeping, even Ron in his watch chair on the first floor, an old pipe in the Bonny Hall basement boiler room cracked, leaking, then broke. Water poured out in a torrent, making a mess that would soon become a flood.

TWELVE

Pria and Maya both yawned and stretched and shivered in the exact same way. Realizing what they had just done they laughed and raced to the communal bathroom. As usual they were up before any of the other students. Maya turned on the faucet. Nothing came out.

"Uh oh."

Pria, who had paused to gaze out the window at the snow, turned, "Uh-oh what?"

"No water."

"It snowed last night."

Maya joined her sister at the window. "Oh boy. We need to find Shin."

"Yeah. No showers or toilets." Pria shrugged. "That's what the honey pots are for. Mrs. Hood was right. But that means the pipes froze last night."

The two of them hurried back to their room to dress and hunt down Shin, the one person they knew could solve just about any maintenance issue.

* * *

Nurse Krenshaw stood in the makeshift infirmary next to the desk she'd converted into a nurse's station. She had not slept well, too keyed up over what Shin might find out about Kimberly and Michael. She had expected him to come back to her when he was done doing whatever he usually did. Unfortunately, he had not. Now, here she was, waiting, and listening to the faint, echoing sounds of students waking up. She paced the room to get her blood moving and to ward off the chill.

"Nancy."

She jerked in surprise, turning towards the door at the unexpected sound of Shin's voice. "Shin! You startled me."

"My apologies. I wanted to speak with you before the children woke." He moved into the infirmary. "I found Michael. Dead."

Nancy's eyes widened. "How?"

"Suicide. Drugs. Alcohol."

"And Kimberly?" Nancy didn't want to think of what might have happened to her friend.

Shin shook his head. "I don't know. I haven't found her. At least, not in the Admin building or Hadfield Hall. I need to do a more thorough search to see if—"

"If he killed her." Nancy debated again about telling Shin the whole truth.

Shin turned and gaze up at the ceiling, his impassive face frowning. Nancy tilted her head. Then she heard it: running feet down the stairs. She picked up her baton. Shin shifted into a ready stance. There wasn't any screaming, just running. But running right now could mean danger.

Maya and Pria skidded to a halt in the doorway, eyes going wide at the tenseness of the two adults. The girls ducked their heads and Maya stepped behind Pria.

"I trust you have a good reason for acting like a herd of wild elephants." Nancy's voice was stern with disapproval.

"Yes, Nurse Krenshaw. We're sorry," Pria said. "But we came looking for you to find Shin. The water isn't working and it snowed last night."

It took a moment for Nancy and Shin to process what the student said and what she actually meant. Finally, Shin asked, "Have you seen flooding?"

The girls shook their heads.

"The basement." Nancy made shooing motions at them. "Girls, you help him if it's what we all think it might be."

Shin nodded to Nancy and headed off towards the basement stairs with the sisters trailing after. As they left Julie hurried into the infirmary.

Nancy took a breath. "I know about the water. It's being looked into."

Julie shook her head in confusion. "Toni and Rose are sick. So's Aaron and Shane." The redhead shifted uncomfortably. "They all spent the night together in Toni's room. I went there to borrow a shirt and she wouldn't let me in. Told me she thought they all had the flu."

"Oh goodness gracious. Isn't this just the way of things?" Nancy began gathering medicine and supplies in a pack. "We'll leave them in there for now. If they've infected Toni's room, we might as well contain it to that."

"You aren't mad?"

Nancy gave the girl a knowing look. "Who do you think has been giving them condoms all this time? No. I'm not mad. Mrs. Hood on the other hand…"

Julie flushed at the thought.

If she'd still alive. Nancy pushed the thought away and followed Julie to Toni's room.

* * *

They could hear the rushing of water the moment Shin opened the basement door. "Damn." Shin gestured to the sisters. "Wait here. I'm going to turn off the water from the outside." He sprinted back up the stairs, leaving them behind.

Maya opened the basement door and saw that the building foundation must have a slight slope to it. She could see water stretch across the basement hall floor, filling the west end of the building, and all its rooms, including the root cellar, the boiler room, the honey pot room and loading area. The water was still about five feet from this end of the building.

Pria poked her head in and wrinkled her nose. "This is going to suck. Maybe we can get the rest in the building to help fix it. After all, we all need to use the honey pot."

The sound of running, splashing water cut off, signaling that Shin had found the main water cutoff and had successfully used it.

"Maybe. I hope so." Maya looked at the dark water, reflecting the faint early morning light. "And I hope there's nothing, you know, *floating* in it. I don't smell anything but still."

"Ew. You think of the nastiest things." Pria threw her long ponytail over her shoulder. "You'd better hope there's nothing in that."

* * *

Nancy surveyed the sick foursome in Toni's room with something akin to resignation. Three months without a serious illness had been a godsend. Now, as Julie and Sophia helped set up the twin bed mattresses on the floor for those who did not officially live in this room, Nancy examined each of her patients. Fever, nausea, sweats, headache, and body aches. All classic signs of the flu. It might be a bad cold but those don't usually come with nausea and vomiting. Then again, it could be a hangover from the size of the empty rum bottle. Things were going to get a lot worse if diarrhea hit, especially with a busted water pipe.

As each student was tucked into bed, Nancy considered moving the lot of them over to Hadfield Hall. It, after a quick inspection by Shin, still had water and sound water pipes. As it was, Shin was spending his morning with John and Ken wrapping water pipes and turning off water to the buildings they weren't using.

"Gloves in the trash. Keep the face masks and use hand sanitizer as soon as you're clear. You two are on watch duty for the day if one of them needs to use the restroom. You'll have to escort them down to the honey pots." Nancy flapped a hand at the girls, wishing Athena were here as she swallowed her grief anew. Athena would've jumped to deal with this. "Figure out the schedule yourselves and rope John and Ken into it for the evening."

The girls nodded and took off. Nancy heard Julie ask as they headed down the hallway, "Where's the nearest comfy chair we can move?"

She turned back to her charges. "You four are in a pickle. I'm not going to scold you for anything you did but I will tell you that you're in for one hell of crappy week or two if this really is the flu instead of a heavy duty cold. If you need to throw up, use the buckets, for heaven's sake!" Nancy frowned at the weak choir of acknowledgment. "Julie or Sophia will be outside. I'll give you more medicine in four hours. Until then you are not to get out of bed."

"Don't worry, Nurse K," Toni mumbled. "I don't wanna go anywhere." The rest mumbled or grunted agreement.

Nancy shook her head as she left the dorm room, closing the door behind her.

* * *

Within twelve hours Lee and Melissa were both sick—sweating, headache, and nausea. There was no doubt Melissa was infected as well. Whether it was through her mouth, her nose, or her eyes, some of the zombie's blood had penetrated her body and done its damage.

Joe, Heather, Nicholas, and Rachel huddled together as far away from the infected pair as they could. Ostensibly it was to give the couple privacy to say goodbye to each other and to make peace with God. In truth, it was the fear of being infected as much as for the privacy.

"What are we going to do?" Rachel's voice was small and broken.

"What we need to do." Joe took a breath. "And what they need to do. Lee will take care of Melissa, and then take care of himself. I'm going to be the one to make sure it sticks."

"It? You mean murder, right?" Though still soft, her voice had a note of hysteria in it.

Joe gave Nicholas a hard look.

Nicholas pulled Rachel closer and murmured in her ear, "It's not murder. They're already dead. They probably don't have even another day in them. The virus, the infection, whatever the hell it is, it works fast. This has to happen."

Rachel buried her face in Nicholas' shoulder, her whole body shaking hard against his.

Lee raised his voice, rough with fatigue and pain. "We're ready."

Heather swallowed hard. "I'm going to check upstairs. See if the zombies are still there or if they have wandered off."

Joe squeezed her hand and let her go. He sat there for a moment before he stood and walked over to Lee and Melissa. They were sitting on the floor as far away from the stairs and the door as they could get. Lee had his back against the wall with Melissa between his legs, curled up against his chest. She didn't look up as Joe approached. Lee did. He gave Joe a wan smile. "This is it. I don't want to wait too much longer. I want to make sure I can control the pistol."

"Heather's making sure the coast is clear. Then we'll go upstairs and wait." Joe cleared his throat. "You should use my 9mm. It's the quietest of the pistols we have and packs a punch." He rubbed his mouth while he said this, feeling like a heel for wanting to keep the noise to a minimum.

"Good idea."

Heather moved quietly back down the stairs to the halfway point. "Pretty clear. We're probably going to have to deal with one or two as we leave but they've mostly wandered off again. Uh, and it's snowed. Like, for real." She gave Joe a pleading look before she turned and fled back upstairs.

Joe ignored the news about the snow and read the look for what it was: a request for him to get her stuff and not make her go back down into the dark. "Okay everyone. Get your things

and the supplies we found. We're heading to the bunker shortly."
He watched as Nicholas and Rachel gathered their things, taking
the bulk of the supplies and leaving Heather's for him. Once
they were gone Joe gathered up the rest of the stuff, blinking
away the burning tears that flooded his eyes.

He gave up the pretense of stoicism as he returned to Lee and
Melissa, tears flowing down his face. He tried to speak and failed.

Lee offered him his hand. "It's been a good run. You'll get
them to safety. I know you will."

Joe gripped Lee's hand tight. "I will. I promise." Then he
pressed his 9mm pistol into Lee's hand. "Safety's off."

The two of them stared at each other for a long moment,
then Lee nodded. Joe nodded back. He turned to the stairs,
wiping at his face. He didn't look back.

*   *   *

Lee held the semi-automatic down by his side as he petted
Melissa's hair with his injured arm. When the wound in the
arm had stopped hurting and the general aches started he knew
deep in his bones he was done. Melissa looked up at him, then
kissed him like the dying woman she was, and murmured, "I
love you" to his lips.

"I love you, Mel. I really do. More than life itself." He
squeezed her tight, raised the weapon, waited for her to close
her eyes, and pulled the trigger.

*   *   *

Joe continued to wipe at his face as he closed the basement
door. He joined the other three in the living room. They were
clustered together in the center, holding each other. Joe joined
them, bowing his head to press against theirs as they all mourned
their loss.

The first shot, while not loud, was like a hammer to the heart. They jerked as one. The second shot came shortly after. Then the third. They continued to hold each other, silent except for their tears.

Finally, Joe raised his head. "Nicholas, Rachel…scout the windows downstairs. Heather, upstairs. I got one last thing to do." His face was still wet but his eyes were dry and gritty as he hardened his heart and his mind to do what needed doing. He had a promise to keep.

* * *

Caleb ducked into the temporary Bonny Hall room that Ron and Jeff shared. "You seen Steve? I don't think he came back after you guys pulled watch."

"He didn't?" Ron sat on his bed with his back to the wall. He watched the snow drifting down in big, fat flakes. Next to him was the book he'd taken. "Perhaps he needed some alone time to think on his sins."

Caleb stiffened, then closed the door to the room. "What do you mean? What sins?" His voice lowered, his lip curled in anger. "If you're talking about how me and Steve are—"

"I couldn't give two shits about who's fucking who," Ron interrupted.

"Then what sins are you talking about?"

"The same sin I think you're suffering from."

Caleb paused, the hair on the back of his neck rising in fear. "I don't understand. What's happened to Steve?"

Ron turned from the window and gazed impassively at Caleb. "His lack of faith in Jeff and Jeff's plan to make sure we all survive the winter."

"If you've hurt him—"

Ron was off the bed, across the room, and had slammed Caleb up against the door before he realized what was happening. Caleb felt the cold metal of Ron's knife against the side of his throat as the taller boy leaned his weight on the arm pressing against Caleb's chest.

"You'll what? I could kill you six ways from Sunday before you raised a hand against me. Shit, you don't even have a weapon on you, knowing there are zombies inside the walls. You'll do nothing."

For a moment Caleb couldn't breathe. He stared into Ron's eyes and saw the madness he and Steve had always suspected lurking there. "My bat is in my room." Then he shoved Ron away from him...or tried to. Ron pressed harder, forcing air from his lungs. "Stop," Caleb's demand came out as a wheeze.

Ron leaned in close, almost nose to nose with Caleb. He smiled a fierce, savage grin. "Leaving your weapon behind was your second mistake. Your first was challenging me. Do it again and I'll kill you." He let Caleb go and backed up two steps. "I swear it. You live by my will alone. Now, maybe you want to go think on your sins so you don't end up like Steve. Jeff doesn't need either of you."

Caleb stared at Ron and realized he meant what he said... and that he must've murdered Steve during their watch shift. Caleb opened the door and backed out without taking his eyes off of Ron and his savage grin that begged for Caleb to attack.

Instead, Caleb closed the door quietly and turned away, trying to figure out what to do next. It was possible that Steve wasn't dead. Maybe he'd just had a bad night in Ron's company and chose to return to Hadfield. Maybe. Caleb hoped it was so but didn't believe it for a minute. Either way he needed to check.

* * *

"This is the worst thing I've ever had to do," Maya declared as she soaked the mop in the flood water and rung it out the bucket.

Pria mirrored her action with her own mop and bucket. "No kidding. You'd think that the rest would help but no, use the honey pot and run."

"Aaron and them are sick."

"Jeff is getting food ready for lunch."

"Sophia and Julie are watching the sick people." Maya stopped and stretched. "Everyone's too busy to help. Of course." She picked up rolled the bucket down the up hall to the one room with the drain. Silently she snarled at the crappy construction of putting a drain at the top of a sloped foundation. If it were at the bottom they wouldn't be cleaning up this mess. Then again the architects probably didn't plan to put the laundry room at the top of a slope or to have a slope at all. At least they had a drain in the laundry room in anticipation of broken washers. Maya poured out the water, watching it swirl away, thankful there was nothing more than water and a little dirt in it.

"And where is Mrs. Hood, anyway? Or Professor Leeds?" Pria paused and made a face at Maya. "You don't think they're *together*. Do you?"

Shin cut off any answer Maya might have made as he entered the basement. Maya returned to the flooded area to stand next to her sister. The two of them waited for Shin to approach. He looked around and nodded. "You do good work. No one else is helping you?"

Pria shook her head. "Aaron, Toni, Rose, and Shane are sick. Sophia and Julie are watching them. Jeff is cooking. John and Ken were off with you." She paused. "I think Caleb, Steve, and Ron are all patrolling for zombies."

Shin considered this. "I sent John and Ken to assist Jeff with lunch. Nurse Krenshaw is keeping an eye on the sick ones, most likely." He glanced away, then looked each sister in the eye. "My apologies. I cannot stay and help you. I need to find Mrs. Hood."

The sisters looked at each other. "And Professor Leeds?" Pria asked.

He hesitated then gave her a single nod. "And Professor Leeds."

Maya spoke up. "They didn't run away together...did they?"

"No." Shin shook his head. "I don't believe so. Nevertheless, I must find them. I've already given Hadfield and the Admin building a look. Now I go to search the grounds, the sheds, and the other outlying buildings. It is possible they are out there, in the fire watchtower, or the foundation of the astronomy tower. If I don't find them... Tomorrow I will be more thorough in my building-to-building search." He gazed at the dark water. "Take a break to eat lunch. It's important to clean this up before it freezes or molds but your health is more important."

"Yes, Shin." The sisters said at the same time, then grinned at each other.

Shin cracked a smile, then turned and left the basement.

The two of them watched him go. Maya's gaze lasted longer on the closed door as she asked, "You get the feeling that he was hiding something?"

Pria, already back at work, shrugged. "Yes. But, of the faculty, I trust him second only to Mrs. Hood."

Maya turned back to her work without a word, wondering what had had happened to Mrs. Hood and Professor Leeds.

* * *

Jeff patrolled the Commons inside and out. This was his domain. From the no longer functioning walk-in freezer to the half-full pantry to the industrial kitchen and the dining hall, the Commons belonged to him. After locking the back entrance to the kitchen and ensuring there was only one way in and out through the front he got to work on lunch. Less people did mean less food to prepare.

Three faculty and fourteen students, four of whom were so ill that Nurse Krenshaw requested that he figure out a way to make broth for them. She didn't ask how he would do it. She just knew that he would figure it out. Jeff felt the warmth of being needed and depended upon.

Seventeen people. Jeff looked at his list of supplies and worried his bottom lip. They might make it through the winter with only seventeen to feed. With the snow he was certain the supply run team wouldn't make it back, or wouldn't make it back with the listed supplies. As Jeff dug into the walk-in pantry, looking for what he needed in order to make lunch, a thought came to him.

Four people on the supply run. Four people sick. As it stood, the pantry could feed the seventeen of them through the winter. There'd be some rationing and some creative cooking but they would survive. Jeff felt the pulsing of the panic that had gripped him off and on for the last week lessen. The fear of starvation and watching those he actually cared about dying around him.

But only if it were no more than seventeen. The supply team might make it back. Might. And he owed Lee for what he did to him without warning. Jeff worried his bottom lip more, then decided. Four for four. It was more than a fair exchange. Lee, Joe, Melissa, and Nicholas were worth more and worked harder than the sick ones. Jeff nodded to himself, decided.

He returned to the kitchen, already warmer with the wood stove aflame, and searched through the cleaning supplies stored in neat rows on the rack above the sink. To the far right were the poisons: ant, roach, and rat. Rat poison would be a perfect addition to the broth. It would only kill only those four students because the broth was only for them.

Jeff turned around and suppressed a jump as he saw Ron standing there. He hadn't heard his friend come in. "Hey." He continued over to the woodstove where he had five cups of water and powdered broth cooking.

"Interesting spice."

"Isn't it?"

Ron licked his lips with a quick flick of his tongue. "Who's it for?"

Jeff glanced at Ron out of the corner of his eye and was pleased to see admiration and adoration in his friend's face. "The sick ones. Four of them. Four people on the supply run. We have enough to feed only seventeen."

Ron looked up and left as he calculated. "Fair enough." He paused, then added. "Caleb's gonna come see you."

"Why?"

"Because he thinks I killed Steve."

Jeff gave Ron a sharp look. "Did you?"

"Yes." Ron shrugged. "He was going to deny you when the supply run came back. Deny you like Peter denied Jesus. I thought he should think on the error of his ways."

"Don't think he'll be thinking on anything if he's dead." Jeff kept his voice light with an effort. Inside he was quaking. Ron had killed again and one of their friends this time. He'd liked Steve. *They both had,* he thought.

"And he won't be denying anyone now." Ron moved closer. "What's for lunch?"

Jeff didn't know what to make of Ron's murder-happy descent. But as long as Ron was murdering for him he'd deal with it. "Lunch is a pack of nuts, a pack of crackers, and a selection of apocalypse burritos." An apocalypse burrito was canned meat, like tuna or chicken, served in a tortilla.

"I get spam." Ron smiled and suddenly, he was the childhood friend Jeff had always known.

"All right." Jeff relaxed and smirked. "Your wish, my command.

CHAPTER
THIRTEEN

Y eah, this looks like something a wealthy, paranoid prepper would create for the apocalypse." Heather shivered in the cold. They had been surprised by the two inches of snow that covered the ground when they'd left Lee and Melissa behind. "Too bad for them they went hunting."

"Good for us," Joe said, rubbing his hands. "Nicholas, Rachel, I'm going to need you to boost me up. Just to look over the wall to see what I can see." The two of them moved over to him and offered Joe their clasped hands as footholds, allowing him a good look at the empty yard with its pristine snow cover and, more importantly, that the top of the stone wall was covered with imbedded chunks of sharp glass. "Lemme down."

"Zombies?" Rachel brushed her hands clean of mud and muck. She kept her voice low, despite the fact that the cold seemed to have slowed the zombies down.

"Not that I could see. Problem though. Glass shards on top of the wall. We need something to cover it so we can get over the wall without cutting ourselves."

Nicholas raised a finger as he opened his mouth, then paused and shook his head. He tried again with the same result. The third time he smiled as he raised his finger, "The car, the one with the smashed window, we could use the floor mats."

As one, the four of them looked back towards the car that had crashed into the backyard they'd just come from. It was one of the few yards without a fence and it looked like the driver had tried to drive through in order to escape. They failed but they appear to have gotten away. There was no gore or dried blood around the car. Just a couple of smashed windows.

"Good idea. We need at least two. More if they're there. I'm going to have to stay up on the wall to help the rest of you over and I don't fancy glass in my ass." Joe managed a half-smile. No one responded with more than a brief smile as Nicholas and Rachel returned to the car to get the rubber floor mats. There were only two to get. Nicholas shrugged as they returned and offered them up.

The four of them juggled getting the mats in place, then Joe on top, straddling the wall, to grab Heather as she was boosted up, then help her down. She was the shortest of them and had the longest to drop at about two-and-a-half feet. She winced as she hit the ground and tumbled but waved off Joe's visible concern. Heather was on her feet and helping Rachel, then Nicholas down to the ground. Joe shifted his position and looked down at the ground. He decided caution was the better part of valor and lowered himself down instead of jumping.

All four of them shivered as they waited, listening and watching. There was no movement and no sound. Joe signaled them to move for the back door under a covered patio. They hurried in a group. Joe grabbed the doorknob and swore almost soundlessly. He showed that the door was locked. Heather dug into her coat and pulled out a small leather fold. She opened up the flap with a waggle of her eyebrows, revealing a set of shiny lockpicks.

"Really?" he mouthed at her as he moved aside to let her at the door.

Heather whispered with a half-smirk, "Detective's daughter. Taught me a lot of things a nice young lady shouldn't know." Then she went to one knee, putting her lockpicking skills to work. It took her about five minutes and some soundless swearing to get the job done. The whole time Rachel and Nicholas stood guard, watching the yard and the sides of the house, waiting for zombies to attack. Joe stayed by Heather's side, watching her and listening to the inside of the house.

When Heather stood Joe clicked his tongue once, calling them together in a huddle. "Clear the house. Every single room and closet. Every single door gets opened. First floor. Then second." Everyone nodded. "Order: Me, Heather, Rachel, Nicholas." He waited for unanimous agreement, then straightened and turned to the back door.

The house was large, practically a mansion, and smelled mostly of stale air and some decay. Not much, though. It was a good sign. They cleared each room on the first floor, only pausing to look at the door that could only be reached by going through the walk-in pantry that was more of a hallway than enclosed room. The pantry, to everyone's pleasure, was fully stocked with non-perishables.

"That's probably the entrance to the bunker," Rachel said after conferring with Heather. "Gina used to talk about Todd and his prepper friends. Most of them were pretty rabid."

Joe considered this. "Let's clear the rest of the house first, then we'll come back to this. Better safe than sorry. And if there are zombies down there we'll just lock them in until we can deal with them."

The upstairs revealed two bedrooms, a bathroom, a master suite with its own bathroom, and a storage room with more emergency gear. But no zombies. Nicholas shook his head. "Preppers, man. Why multiple rooms of stuff?"

"So you have stuff upstairs if your house floods or if the first floor is compromised. Didn't you see how this half of the house could be cut off from the rest? The door at the top of the stairs?" Rachel pointed out the metal bar and doorstop. "I'll bet the door is metal or has a metal core."

Heather and Joe joined them in the hallway. "I bet," Heather said, "that this is a custom built house. If there's a well it's in the basement or the bunker."

"Custom or not, it's ours now." Joe headed down the stairs. "Time to see what's behind door number three."

* * *

The door at the other end of the pantry turned out to be a staircase down to basement unlike anything any of them had ever seen. It was more of a third level to the house than a basement, completely underground with low level lights that automatically turned on. The lights startled everyone for a moment before they nodded to each other, realizing they were motion activated. It was a safe bet that no one was down there. However, they cleared each room as they came to it.

This third floor was fully paneled, furnished, and broken out into four rooms: a romper room with pool table, couches, and an entertainment center, a pseudo kitchen and bar, a large bathroom complete with water pump, and a weapons room with more guns and ammunition than Joe had ever seen in any private collection as along with other military equipment.

It was completely devoid of people and zombies alike.

Joe stopped to look at the weapons as the rest split up to look at the wonders of the other rooms. Rachel and Nicholas returned to the romper room to look at the books and videos. Rachel, paused by the bookshelf and pointed at the red light on the cord connected to the TV. "It's got electricity."

Nicholas hunkered down to look at the cord and its blocky plug-in. "It's an energy saver. The light says there's electricity but you need to hit this button to turn on power to the TV itself."

"Wild."

"Running water," Heather called from the bathroom. "Sink and pump. Really cold water." She turned to the closet's partially open folding door and opened it fully.

Joe walked over to where Rachel and Nicholas stood, looking at a small bookcase filled with prepper books. "I don't get it. If this is the bunker where's the food? Where's the sleeping room?"

Nicholas and Rachel looked at each other. "Don't know. Maybe the whole house is considered to be the bunker?"

"Guys!" Heather's excited voice called. "I think I found the bunker door. I—" Her voice cut off as a loud click, followed by a swishing sound, came from the bathroom.

"Heather!" Joe ran to the bathroom door. He was greeted by Heather slowly turning as she looked down at an arrow protruding from the right side of her stomach.

* * *

"As duties go, this one's pretty light." Julie, wrapped in a blanket, was snuggled down in the loveseat they had dragged up from the first floor lobby. "Escort them to the bathroom, help give them medicine. I haven't heard anything out of them since about two o'clock. They had lunch and their medicine. Otherwise we leave them alone."

Sophia, perched on the edge of the loveseat in a heavy coat, shrugged. "Nurse Krenshaw told us to work out the watch schedule. That's basically what we're telling you guys. You get the evening shift."

John and Ken looked at each other, then at the girls. "Really? All night?" Ken asked.

"Probably. But you'll have to ask Nurse Krenshaw when she shows up for the six o'clock medicine." Sophia exchanged a glance of confirmation with Julie who shrugged. "Isn't that when you're going to get dinner for them?"

John sighed and nodded. "I just don't like sick people. They…" He trailed off.

"Make you nervous? Like they're zombies?" Ken supplied. "Yeah. Me, too."

"C'mon. Kitchen duty. Don't imagine it's going to be any different than normal but don't want to get Jeff annoyed at us." John tapped Ken's shoulder, then waved to the girls.

"Hey," Julie called as they waved back. "Have dinner with us? Watch duty doesn't have to suck. Company is always appreciated and they won't miss us for half an hour."

Ken paused and nodded. "Sure. See you then." He and John exchanged a pleased grin as they heard Sophia and Julie giggling with each other.

* * *

Jeff sent the basket of food for Bonny Hall off with John and Ken. Tonight's dinner was a treat: fried peanut butter and fluffernutter sandwiches on flour tortillas. It was basically dessert but he knew none of the students, or even the faculty, would complain. Sweets were becoming a rare treat. The usual crackers and nuts would be an added, regular bonus.

He was cleaning up the mess when Caleb came bursting into kitchen. Jeff spun, grabbing the nearest weapon at hand, a large butcher knife, brandishing it before he realized it was his friend.

"Whoa!" Caleb pulled up short, raising his hands. "It's me."

"What the hell, Caleb? You trying to get killed?"

"No. I can't find Steve and I think Ron killed him and I found Mrs. Hood. It was supposed to look like suicide but it wasn't. I'm pretty sure it was Ron."

Jeff lowered the knife but didn't put it away. "Wait. What? Slow down."

Caleb made the effort to control his racing thoughts. "Steve didn't come back from watch with Ron last night. When I asked him about it he implied that he killed Steve and that he'd kill me if he wanted to. I didn't believe him. So, I spent the day going through Hadfield Hall. I opened every single door I could, thinking that, maybe, Ron had scared him and he was hiding…or maybe Ron had hidden his body somewhere." He took a breath. "I found Mrs. Hood. She was on the fourth floor, tucked deep in a closet. It was supposed to look like suicide. Her wrists were slit but there was no knife. And there was blood on the wall behind her, like she'd been hit in the head. It was Ron. It had to be."

"She was on the list." Jeff kept his voice calm as he walked over to Caleb. "Second on the list after Swenson."

Caleb stared at him, disbelief and outrage warring for dominance on his face. "Did you...?"

"Does it matter? Would it change your anger if I was the one who had killed her? She *was* on the list."

"But Steve wasn't!"

Jeff shook his head. "No. He wasn't. Are you sure he's dead?"

"Have I found the body? No. But, yeah, I think he's dead. He hasn't been seen all day and Ron implied he was dead." Caleb closed his eyes. "You've got to do something about him."

"Ron?"

"Yeah."

"Do what?" Jeff tilted his head. "Kill him?"

"Yes. No. I don't know. Maybe. He's killing people who aren't on the list."

Jeff bowed his head. "I think he's right. You really would turn on us in a heartbeat." He looked Caleb in the eye. "You would betray me after everything." Before Caleb could answer Jeff slashed his childhood friend's throat, cutting an artery and spraying blood across the kitchen

Ron, who had crept up behind Caleb, pulled the struggling boy over to the deep, industrial sized kitchen sink and forced his head down so the sink caught most of the blood pulsing from Caleb's throat. Ron had no trouble keeping Caleb's head down as the boy struggled to stand and stanch the blood flow at the same time. "You know, I didn't think you had it in you. You haven't actually killed anyone close up until now."

Jeff, looking at his reflection in the bloody knife, shrugged. "I didn't know I did either. I've known Caleb for as long as I can remember." He pulled his gaze from the knife. "But, you're right, he'd cracked. Killing Steve broke him. He would've told everyone of our plans."

Ron had the grace to look chagrined. "I said I was sorry. I can't help it if I'm overprotective of you."

Jeff grimaced as he realized the extend of the blood spray. "What a mess. Ah, well. What else am I going to do? I'm good at cleaning up messes."

"Yeah. I'll take care of the body."

* * *

Julie and Sophia passed Ken and John in the hallway. Ken had a tray of covered bowls while John carried the rest of dinner. "Don't forget, dinner in the front lobby. We'll meet you there after we feed the sickies." John lifted his tray up. "Peanut butter and fluffernutter!"

"Really? You better make sure there's some left." Sophia called over her shoulder. "I gotta help Nurse Krenshaw with the medicine."

"Yeah, yeah."

Sophia elbowed Julie as they headed down the stairs. "That goes for you too. Make sure I get some. Peanut butter's my favorite."

Julie grinned. "I just won't call for Pria or Maya until after you and the boys get back."

"Sounds like a plan." Sophia split off from her friend and headed the makeshift infirmary as Julie continued to the first floor lobby.

* * *

John put his bat on the loveseat and opened Toni's dorm room door. Both boys recoiled at the smell of sweat and sickness that boiled out the room at them. "Damn," John muttered. He raised his voice as Ken entered before him with the broth. "Dinner time, guys. More broth and Jeff made us a treat for dinner." Aaron was standing at the window, looking out. The rest of them were still in bed but moving slowly. He closed the door, waiting for Ken to get over to the tray next to Rose and Shane on the floor.

Talking as he walked over to Aaron, John offered up one of the wrapped tortillas. "It's peanut butter and fluffernutter." He paused, catching the acrid stink of sweat from standing so close to Aaron. "If you want, we can crack the window and get some fresh air in here. It'll be cold but—"

Whatever else John was going to turned into a yell of pain and surprise as Aaron turned and lunged, grabbing John and sinking his teeth into John's neck. Aaron ripped off a large chunk of flesh and swallowed it whole.

Ken straightened and turned at John's first yell. "Shit. Oh, shit." He spun for the door but was blocked by Toni. Then Shane and Rose had him by the legs and were trying to bite through his jeans to get at his flesh. He couldn't keep his balance as Toni grabbed at him, pulling him towards her questing mouth. John went down in a tumble. He didn't have a chance to scream before the three zombies had found their marks.

* * *

"Is it good?" Sophia smiled at Nurse Krenshaw as she tucked into the tortilla sandwich and washed the bite down with some water.

Nancy nodded and wiped her mouth with an almost guilty gesture. "Yes. Like heaven. Ought to put me into a diabetic coma."

"You have diabetes?"

The nurse shook her head. "No, no. Just, it's so sweet. Come in." She pointed to another napkin wrapped tortilla. "Help yourself. Have a little dinner before we go up. I was saving that for later but I can go get another one. The boys said that Jeff made enough to feed an army."

Sophia shook her head with a shy smile. "Nah, me and Julie are going to eat dinner with Ken and John."

Nancy saw Sophia's flush. "Ooh. Which one do you fancy?"

"Ken."

"Such a nice boy." The nurse stood with a small groan. "Well, then. Let's get our things and get you on your way. Wouldn't want you late for your date."

The two of them walked down the first floor hallway and up to the second floor. Sophia stopped Nurse Krenshaw in the stairwell. "Uh, I was wondering. Julie said…" Sophia flushed. "She said you weren't mad about Toni and Rose being with Aaron and Shane because you were the one to give them condoms." Sophia stared at the brown bottle of cough medicine in her hand. "Could I? Do you have more?"

Nancy tilted Sophia's chin up so she could make eye contact. "Yes. I have more condoms. Yes, you may have as many as you and Julie need." When she was sure Sophia wasn't going to look away, Nancy removed her hand. "I'll show you where they are. I'd rather you were all safe with each other." She tilted her head. "You never need to be embarrassed about your body or your needs with me. I was quite the wild child in my day. There's little you can do that will surprise me. Please let the other girls know this."

Sophia glanced away, and then back at Nancy's face. "Okay. I will. Thank you."

Nancy gave a mental sigh of relief. She didn't know what had happened to Mrs. Hood but she could only assume the worst. With Leeds out of the picture—*Thank God!*—it was up to her and Shin to lead the children as best they could. She needed to know they trusted her. It was only way she could make sure they were as well as they could be.

Sophia opened Toni's door and fell back with a cry of panic. "Zombies!" She threw the bottle of cough syrup at Toni but it didn't stop the dead student from capturing Sophia's arm to keep her from fleeing. Shane squeezed himself through the door to tackled both Toni and Sophia to the ground.

Nancy backed away, feeling a sharp pain in her chest and her arm. She stumbled to the stairwell door and through it, dropping her bag of medicines. All she could think to do was get away, to keep moving. She knew she was moving too slow. She knew, as she clutched her left arm, she was having a heart attack. Nancy's foot slipped as one of the zombies followed her down.

Tumbling down the concrete stairs with small yelps and groans of pain she wondered what would kill her first: the zombie, the stairs, or her heart. She was surprised when she stopped at the bottom and was still alive. She could barely move but she was still alive. Crawling, Nancy made it to, and halfway through, the first floor door. Behind her a zombie tumbled down the stairs after her.

"Julie." Her voice was so weak. "Julie. Help!"

Julie looked up from her reading and saw Nurse Krenshaw on the floor halfway out of the back stairwell. "Holy shit!" She dropped her book and sprinted down the hallway to help the old woman. Julie skidded to a halt and went to her knees and grabbed the nurse's bloody hand. "Nurse Krenshaw! Oh, God. Tell me what to do. Did you fall? What—?"

Nancy's gasp of pain cut off Julie's frantic questions. Julie saw movement through the door, looked, and realized Shane was tearing away hunks of Nurse Krenshaw's calf with his teeth. Nurse Krenshaw exhaled audibly and stopped moving altogether. The zombie looked at Julie and started scrabbling over the nurse's unmoving body in slow, clumsy movements. Julie saw that both its legs were bent at the wrong angle.

She did the only thing she could think to do: she pushed and kicked at the nurse's body until it cleared the door, closing the zombie into the stairwell.

* * *

Shin looked at his watch lunch had come and gone many hours ago. It was dinner time and the sun was fast moving towards the horizon. Much of the land he'd covered was already in shade. Like the daylight, Shin's mood was growing dim. He had looked everywhere he could think of on the walled grounds of the academy. From the fire watchtower that was a frequent student trysting spot to the guard shacks on both the front and back campus entrances to the beginning construction of the astronomy tower to the garden shed at the farthest point of the wall where he sat now.

If Kimberly was still on campus she was well hidden…and most likely dead. Shin could not imagine a woman as forthright as the dorm mistress fleeing at the first sign of danger. The more plausible answer was that Professor Leeds murdered her and got creative with disposing of her body. Still, he had had to check out here because Kimberly had once mentioned coming to this garden shed from time to time to get away from everyone.

The only buildings he hadn't thoroughly searched were the chapel and the gymnasium. Tomorrow he would search the former and figure out a way to examine the latter from the roof. It was still possible that Mrs. Hood had entered the gymnasium in hopes of rescuing a student or in determination of killing the zombies therein. Shin did not want to think about having accidentally locked the dorm mistress in the building with zombies.

He raised his hand to the sky, putting it under the sun, and saw that the bottom edge of his hand touched the horizon line. About an hour before sunset. He wouldn't make it to the campus until after that.

Suddenly the hair rose on the back of Shin's neck. He looked in the direction of the campus and listened hard. He didn't hear anything but he was so far from campus that he shouldn't hear anything. Still, it felt as if he had heard something…a cry for help? He didn't know. All he knew was that he needed to get back to campus.

Something was very wrong.

CHAPTER
FOURTEEN

Joe rushed in and caught Heather as she fell. She cried out as he jostled the arrow that punctured her low on the right side of her stomach. He looked up at the open closet and saw the small round opening where the arrow shot out next to a door inset in the closet wall.

"Holy crap!" Nicholas moved in to help hold Heather up.

Heather continued to look down at the shaft protruding from the side her abdomen. "It's an arrow."

Joe reached towards the missile but Rachel's sharp command, "Don't touch it!" stopped him cold. Rachel gestured to the boys, "Put her on the floor and don't touch that arrow." She knelt next to her bleeding friend, putting her backpack to the side. "Well, shit. Either she's going to be very lucky or very dead and soon. I need to know what the head of the arrow looks like. See if you two can find out."

Heather swore quietly under her breath.

Nicholas walked over to the closet and looked in. He kept to the left of the open hole. The closet looked like it should hold a washer and dryer set. Instead, it had a couple of slender shelves on either side and the inset door. He looked at the floor and scanned it tile by square tile until he saw the seamed crack. "Okay guys, I'm about to do something stupid. Maybe you want to move out of here."

Rachel shook her head. "Can't. Don't want to move Heather."

"I think I found a pressure plate."

"I got an idea." Joe jumped up, left the bathroom, and returned with a bulletproof vest, a heavy one filled with ceramic plates. He handed it to Nicholas without comment.

"Okay," Nicholas said, "here's the deal. Rachel, you stay flat next to Heather. Joe, you get to the other side of the closet and touch that tile right there when I say 'Go.' I'll hold this up to catch the next arrow. Heather, you stay put."

"I've got a fucking arrow in me! I'm not going anywhere."

Nicholas grinned at her. "There we go, anger to keep the shock at bay." He held the vest about a foot away from the hole. "Go."

Joe pressed the tile. They all heard a click like the one they heard before. An arrow shot out of the hole, bounced against one of the plates in the bulletproof vest, and clattered to the side.

Rachel grabbed the arrow as it stopped moving and held it up. "It's a crossbow bolt. Smooth head. Damn lucky for you." She looked down at Heather. "I think you're going to live. You may not enjoy it but there you go."

Rachel discarded the other bolt, then dug through her backpack for the first aid kit. "This is going to suck but…" She got out the tools she needed.

"Just get it out of me!" Heather's snarl was weak but fierce. "Do what you need to do."

"All right." Rachel reached over and pulled the bolt from Heather's side in a smooth motion. She covered the wound with sterile gauze and medical tape.

Heather yelped, then relaxed as Rachel pulled her hands away. She laid there for a moment, panting softly, getting the pain under control before she asked, "Can we move me to someplace not freezing?"

Rachel nodded. "Yeah. The couch will be fine." She left the bathroom, Joe and Nicholas stepped in and scooped Heather up in a modified basket seat. By the time they got her to the romper room Rachel had blankets waiting. She also had a book in hand. She raised it up. "*When There Are No Doctors*. I saw it on the shelf. I thought it might be a good book to look through right now. I'm hoping the bolt didn't hit any vital organs."

"Sounds like a plan. Let me know if you need anything. Right now, me and Nicholas need to see if we can run that trap out of ammo and then get into whatever is behind that door." He leaned down and kissed Heather on the forehead.

Heather smiled up at him. "But I found it."

"The only thing I want you finding with your body is me. You stay put."

The two of them grinned at each other until Rachel shooed him away. "Go be manly and stuff. But let me know before you open that door. There might be zombies behind it." Rachel pulled her field hockey stick close.

* * *

"Jeff!" Julie yelled as she sprinted from Bonny Hall towards the Commons. She knew Shin was out looking for Mrs. Hood and

Professor Leeds. Of the people she thought she could count on, it was Jeff. He was a natural leader and he'd know what to do. "Jeff!" she yelled again as she burst through the front door of the Commons. "Zombies, Jeff!"

Jeff came out of the kitchen, smelling of pine cleaner. He had his bat in hand. "Where? Here? Where?"

"Bonny Hall. They're in the dorm." Julie collapsed to her knees and started crying. "Nurse Krenshaw…oh God."

"But they're not here? They're not outside?" When Julie didn't answer Jeff hurried to her side and pulled her up by the arm. "Just in Bonny Hall? Nowhere else?"

Julie shook her head. "I don't think so. I didn't see anyone else."

He let go of her arm. "Start at the beginning." Without waiting to see if she would follow him he returned to the kitchen. Once inside he finished up the task he was on, putting away cleaning supplies.

Julie stared after him for a moment and pawed at her tears. She grimaced when she realized that she'd spread some of Nurse Krenshaw's blood on her cheek. With no napkins in sight she wiped her hand on her jeans, then wiped at the blood on her face before she followed Jeff into the kitchen.

"I don't know what happened. I heard Nurse Krenshaw call for help and saw that she'd fallen. She was in the doorway of the stairwell. I thought she'd just had a bad fall. But when I got there Shane was behind her. He was a zombie. He was eating her leg."

Jeff did not look at her as he put the cleaner away and wiped his hands clean with a dish rag. "What then?"

Julie hesitated. "I kicked her body back into the stairwell and ran the other way." She kept her gaze on the tiled floor as she spoke. "That's it. Shane's a zombie. I guess Nurse Krenshaw's one too, now."

"It didn't follow you out?"

"No." Julie glanced up at Jeff.

"Ron! No!" Ron, who had crept up behind Julie, wrapped an arm about her neck and put a 9mm Smith and Wesson pistol to her head. Jeff knew that pistol. It was a twin to the one he had on him. The two of them used to go target shooting all the time. Jeff put his hand in his pocket and stroked the comforting weight of the gun, then clicked the safety to off. "Don't do it."

"Why not?" Ron tightened his grip on her throat. "She's infected. The blood. Don't you see it? If Krenshaw was dead, then the blood's infected. She's dead anyway."

"No. No." Julie squeaked. "She wasn't dead until after I touched her. Jeff, please!"

The plea sounded so much like his sister, Jeff had his pistol out and pointed at Ron before he realized he was going to do it. "Let her go."

Ron stared at Jeff, first with surprise, then with the wounded look of the betrayed. "But she's infected. I'm doing this to save us."

"I'm not." Julie sobbed. "I swear I'm not. The blood, she was alive when I touched it. He bit her after—"

Her words were cut off as Ron tightened his hold on her neck. "I'm doing this for both of us because I have to."

The sound of the guns firing at the same time made it look like Jeff shot both Ron and Julie at the same time. Ron dropped Julie with a bullet through her temple before he crumpled to the floor, a bullet through his forehead. Jeff rushed to them, silent tears springing to his eyes. He touched Julie's red hair, then pulled his hand away.

They were bleeding on his clean floor. There were zombies around. Zombies were drawn to the smell of fresh blood. Jeff stood. He needed to dispose of them. He looked around the kitchen, not really thinking until his eyes fell on the walk-in freezer. It hadn't been opened since the power went out. Most of the frozen meat had been eaten in a hurry or dried into jerky. It was a good enough spot.

Jeff's gorge rose at the fetid smell that wafted out of the air tight room. Instead of placing both bodies neatly as he had planned, he dragged them in just far enough to allow the door to close and dropped them. Closing the freezer door behind him he vomited in the sink, silently swearing never to do that again. He cracked a window to help deal with the lingering miasma and fled to the Commons dining room.

There, he stood, feeling alone, scared, and indecisive. If Shane was a zombie it was a good bet that Aaron, Toni, and Rose were, too. Jeff realized that his poisoned broth had hurried along the inevitable. Now he wondered who was still alive. Ken and John most likely weren't. They delivered the meal. Nurse Krenshaw wasn't. Maybe Sophia. Maybe Pria and Maya. Shin was looking for Mrs. Hood. He shook his head. No. The girls probably weren't still alive. It was probably nothing but zombies over there.

The only way he was going to know was to go and find out. Jeff hesitated even as his hand checked and rechecked his weapons: pistol, bat, knife, collapsible baton. What if he just locked down the doors to Bonny Hall with chain? The zombies wouldn't be able to get out and he had all the food and water here. Those still living, who could escape, could move over to Hadfield Hall or, better yet, turn the Commons into a communal home for the winter.

Jeff nodded to himself. That was best. Lock down Bonny Hall. No one out who wasn't smart enough to get out through the windows would get out, if anyone was left alive. At this point Jeff doubted it. He knew exactly where to get the chains and locks. At least it was something he could still do as things spiraled out of control.

* * *

Pria wiped sweat from her brow as she and Maya closed in on the last of the flood water in Bonny Hall's basement. "They should give us a medal for this." She looked at her abused hands. "Or, at least, some Neosporin."

Standing tall and stretching her back until there was an audible pop, Maya agreed. "No kidding. I don't think this basement's been this clean in ages."

"I'm starved. Shouldn't it be time for dinner?"

Maya nodded. "Yeah. Can't really tell in this light but my stomach says it's time for food."

Pria dropped her mop. "Break time…dinnertime. Whatever." She grabbed her field hockey stick as she headed towards the stairwell at the far end of the hallway. "Coming?"

"Nah." Maya shook her head. "I just want to get this done-done-done. Bring me back something good. I'll finish it up, eat, and then collapse into bed."

"Okay. I'll get you dinner and something for our hands."

Pria ran up the stairs, taking them two at a time. She was tired but it felt good to stretch her legs after spending the entire day mopping up the basement floor and getting rid of the flood water. The scent of peanut butter struck her as soon as she entered the first floor. Following her nose to the lobby she found a stack of napkin wrapped tortillas, packages of crackers, packages of peanuts, and a refilled water dispenser.

For a couple of minutes all Pria did was drink water and eat one of the peanut butter tortillas. It was the best damn thing she'd eaten in forever. Once the first one was gone Pria stuffed four more into the pockets of her coat. She glanced around, looked at the pile of sandwiches left, and stuffed two more into her pockets. She and Maya deserved a little extra after all the work they'd done.

Next, she went to the infirmary, looking for Nurse Krenshaw. She found the room empty. "Where is everyone?" Digging through the basket of supplies Pria found an open tube of Neosporin. She made a note to herself to tell Nurse Krenshaw she took it as she put it in her top pocket.

For a moment she debated going to back to Maya to deliver dinner. Pria shook her head. She needed to figure out where everyone was. If they were having a meeting without her and her sister she wanted to know why. Gripping her hockey stick tighter in sudden wariness and suspicion Pria walked quietly up the central stairs to the second floor. Maybe they were meeting in Toni's room.

She opened the door, stepped into the dimly lit hallway, and froze. There were students wandering about around Toni's door. Students who turned as one to look at the noise and at her. Students who were no longer students.

Pria didn't wait for the zombies to vocalize or to start stumbling towards her. She turned and ran, bolting down the stairs, knowing the second flood doors opened outward and wouldn't hold the zombies for long now that they had the scent of prey. She ran full into the front doors of Bonny Hall, gasping in pain as she rebounded against the barred doors and hit the floor hard. She scrambled to her feet and tried to open the doors again. And couldn't.

With the zombies on their way Pria fled towards one of the side doors at the end of the hallway. She slammed it open and came face-to-face with Nurse Krenshaw. "Zomb—!"

Pria's warning cry was cut off as Nurse Krenshaw thrust herself forward, snapping at Pria's upraised hand. The zombie tore part of Pria's left hand and wrist away before the girl could backpedal. She screamed and hit Nurse Krenshaw in the face as hard as she could with the hockey stick. Turning and sprinting for the other end of the hallway, Pria dodged Rose and Ken, who had already made it to the first floor.

She burst through the double doors at the end and slammed into the outer doors only to find them locked too. She shook the door and saw the chain wrapped around the outside handles. With the zombies still coming there was only one way to go: down into the basement.

Without waiting Pria continued through the heavy single door that bracketed each end of the basement hallway. As soon as she was through she threw the doorstop to keep it from easily being opened. With the door opening outward from the basement, Pria didn't think the zombies could get through that way.

"Pria!" Maya's shout of fear and dismay echoed in the long hallway. "What? What?"

"Get the other door. Block it. Bar it. Keep them out!" While she shouted she took her hockey stick and wedged it into the door handle and against the door. The zombies would have to figure how to pull the door open and have the strength to break the hockey stick if they wanted to get through.

Maya hesitated for the barest of seconds before she sprinted back the way she'd come, grabbing rope from the honey pot room, and splashed through the last of the flood waters up to the basement door. There, she tied one end of the rope to the door handle and the other end to the largest pipe. She stood there for a moment, panting. She froze as she heard *something* on the other side of the door. Backing quietly away Maya returned to the basement hallway.

Pria was standing there, tears flowing down her face as she held a bloody towel to her bleeding hand. "I-I got you some dinner." She hiccupped as she spoke.

"Pria." Maya took a couple of steps closer to her sister.

"You're going to have to pull it out of my right pocket. I don't want to get blood on it or you."

"Pria." She reached for her sister with a trembling hand.

Pria backed away. "I brought you dinner, Maya. And Neosporin. Get them from my coat. Please." Her voice cracked on the last word.

Maya could do nothing but obey. She gingerly slid her hand into Pria's coat pocket and pulled out two napkin wrapped sandwiches then the tube of Neosporin. "I—"

Pria cut her off with a sharp shake of her head. "Don't. I promised Father I'd take care of you. And I'm going to. Until the end." She paused. "Until you end me."

Maya's eyes grew wide and round with shock. "I can't," she whispered.

"You must." Pria's voice was tired but resolved. "I've been bitten. It's the only thing you can do for me now."

* * *

Jeff hurried back to the Commons, his heart full of ice. He closed the doors behind him and walked on numb feet to the kitchen... his domain...his safe haven.

Someone had still been alive in there. Someone had tried to flee through the front doors. He had heard the hit against the chained front door. The desperate shaking. Then silence. Then another hit against a side door and more desperate shaking. He hadn't thought to bring the lock keys or bolt cutters with him. There had been no way to rectify his mistake.

How could he have known? Why didn't they try to go out a window? It had been so obvious to him. Why didn't they just do the obvious thing? Why didn't anyone ever do the obvious thing? When he saw the number of shambling forms through the second floor windows he couldn't get an accurate count. The closest he had gotten was 'more than seven,' which was more than half the number of people he knew still lived when he sent dinner over. When he locked the zombies in it hadn't occurred to him that anyone had survived.

But they had, and he'd, killed them.

How had everything gone so wrong so quickly?

* * *

"Please, please don't make me do this." Tears flowed down Maya's face. "Don't make me kill you. You're the only thing I love in this world."

"If you don't I'm going to kill you when I change." Pria looked down at her hand and took the bloody towel from it. Blood barely dribbled from the gaping wound. "And I'm going to change soon."

Maya started sobbing in great body-shuddering cries. She hunkered down, wrapping her arms around her knees. "I can't kill you. I don't want to live without you. What am I going to do?"

"Get up. Get up." Pria begged as she moved to stand over her sister, not daring to touch her. "Please, Maya. We have to do something." She looked around the hallway until she found what she was looking for. "The root cellar. It has a lock."

Maya looked up at her sister through wet lashes, still crying. She didn't say anything.

"We can lock me up. Put me in there. And figure out what you're going to do next." Pria reached out a hand, then stopped and pulled back into herself. "You've got to live. I promised Father. Let me keep my promise."

This soft plea made Maya nod, stand, and follow Pria to the root cellar. She still carried the two sandwiches. She paused at the door. "Will you eat dinner with me?"

Pria's eyes brightened with tears again as she nodded. "Of course. Once I'm settled." She looked around the dark room, found the little camping lamp Rose used, and flicked it on. "There's the lock they used to keep on the door when it stored more than veggies." Pria pointed at the large rusty lock on the table. "You close and lock the door. I'll bolt it from the inside, too."

Maya put the sandwiches in her coat pocket before she moved to close the door. She looked Pria full in the face. "Your cheek is clean." She stepped forward and planted a soft, trembling kiss on her sister's unmarred skin. "Thank you for being you." Maya stepped back as Pria touched the kiss on her cheek. "I love you."

"I love you, too." Pria nodded for Maya to close the door.

The sobs came again as Maya heard the bolt slide home. She closed the rusted lock with a loud click. "Oh God, Pria…"

"Sit by the door. We'll have dinner." Pria's voice was muffled but audible.

Maya obeyed, pulling the now squished tortilla sandwiches from her pocket. She opened one. "What's the white stuff?"

"I don't know but it's sweet. Let's take a bite at the same time. Okay?"

"Okay."

"One...two...three."

Maya took a bite of the sandwich as Pria spoke the word *three*. It was so sweet and sticky that it was a shock. She didn't know if she should love it or hate it. She chewed slowly, savoring the tastes of the peanut butter and marshmallow cream. "It's... amazing." Energy flooded back into her with the first swallow. She took another, larger bite.

"I know. I know." Pria leaned her head back against the wooden door. "It's like the best parts of a candy bar." She wasn't eating her leftover sandwiches. Just the thought of food made her want to throw up. But she still had the memory of that first sandwich.

The two of them talked while Maya ate both of her sandwiches, making plots and plans on how Maya was going to get out of the basement and to survive with almost everyone dead. Someone was alive. They had to be. Someone chained the doors to Bonny Hall closed.

FIFTEEN

Heather leaned against Joe as the four of them sat around the bunker's table. After exhausting the trap of its ammunition they found the bunker door unlocked. They thought the basement might be a bunker. The prepper's dream they walked down into showed them just how wrong they were. There was an entire one level house down here with everything anyone could want to survive the end of the world.

This included box upon box of emergency food, another pump to the well, an amazing array of drugs, including Percocet. It was what was keeping Heather up at the moment. As well as clothing, books, recharging stations. This prepper wanted to ride out the end of the world in style.

Joe had found books on how to maintain the solar power system installed on the roof of the house. Nicholas found enough beds to house eight people comfortably. Rachel looked through the kitchen and bathroom. Heather found a room painted to look like the outside, complete with park benches, a grill, and a fake sun.

"We need to stay here for the winter. There's no way we can make it back while it's snowing." Joe pet Heather's arm. "And Heather isn't in any shape to move."

"You'll get no argument from me." Rachel sipped the first cold soda she'd had in months and let out a burp with a grin.

Nicholas gazed at his clasped hands. "What about our friends back at the Salton Academy? What do we owe them? I mean, there's enough staples here to get Jeff what he demanded twenty times over. Do we owe it to them to go back with this food?"

Joe was quiet. "I think, if Lee were here, a couple of us might chance it, leaving the rest of you behind."

"No." Heather's voice, though muzzy with drugs, was implacable. "Lee isn't here. You aren't leaving me."

"Vote on it," Rachel said. "All in favor of staying here for at least the winter, say aye."

"Aye." Joe nodded to Rachel.

"Aye," Heather repeated.

"Aye." Rachel looked at Nicholas.

He nodded. "Aye." He raised a hand "But in the spring Joe and I need to take some food back and give our friends the option of coming here. We can take four more people comfortably. Agreed?"

Joe glanced at the boxes. "Agreed. I just wish we could've gotten that medicine for Evan."

"Yeah." Nicholas sighed. It was one of the first things they had looked for when the medical supply was found.

* * *

Dear Jeff,

I don't know if you'll get this letter. I hope you do. I wanted you to know that I waited as long as I could. It's been six weeks now. I haven't eaten anything for three weeks. Just drunk water. Mom's downstairs. I'm too weak to fight her to get to the food. I should've fought her when I still had food and was strong. I was afraid and the thought of killing Mom... I couldn't do it.

I waited for you as long as I could. I'm so hungry and so scared. I waited for you. I did. I tried. I'm so sorry that I'm not strong enough to wait any longer.

I love you, Jeff. You're the best big brother a girl could've ever had. I just wish I could've seen you one last time before the end. Pray for me.

Love,
Kristi

Jeff smoothed the letter of it crinkles as best he could. He missed his little sister so much. He didn't get there in time and it was his fault...all his damn planning. If he'd only gone two days sooner his sister would've been alive. "If wishes were fishes the poor would eat," he murmured.

He hadn't protected his sister...or Julie...or anyone else on campus. The only people who might still be alive were Shin and Professor Leeds. Shin was a good man. Leeds, not so much. But both deserved to live. Jeff just wasn't sure he wanted to live with them. Eventually he would confess his sins and they would kill him themselves.

Or the those returning from the supply run would.

Jeff grimaced, remembering his last conversation with Lee. He shook his head. He was guilty. As guilty as Ron was of killing Julie and Steve. Jeff bowed his head and stared at the letter from his sister. How fitting. He would execute himself for his crimes and join his sister in whatever hell await those who committed suicide.

* * *

"Pria?" Maya waited for some sign that Pria was still awake. "Pria?" Nothing. The tears came again. When Pria woke next, she wouldn't be Maya's sister anymore. Maya got up and moved away from the root cellar door. She didn't want to hear Pria's waking moans as a zombie.

Instead she walked over to the closed elevator doors. When the school had been a functioning school and the world was still alive the elevator had only been for faculty and for students with disabilities. All of the girls used it from time to time to get their laundry to the basement. Of course, when you got caught, it was extra chores for you.

The elevator hadn't worked since the power went out. Now it might be her only saving grace. In the power outage the elevator had automatically moved to the basement floor. Pria's idea was for the Maya to somehow pry open the doors and climb the interior ladder to the fourth floor and get to their prepared shelter. It was as good of a plan as any. If she could get the elevator doors open.

A tapping sound caught her attention. It was soft and rhythmic. She listened. She followed it to another pair of double doors, white knuckling her hockey stick the whole time. It was the first part of "Shave and a Haircut." Her heart leapt. The loading bay doors. She listened for the tapping again. When it came, she answered with the required two taps for two bits.

Maya trembled at the next sound: the heavy click of the doors being unlocked.

The moment Shin came into view Maya threw herself into his arms, burying her face in his shoulder. He made soothing noises, holding her. "Zombies?" He whispered the question in her ear as he looked around for danger.

She nodded. "Locked upstairs…and one in the root cellar."

He pushed her away from him just enough to look at her face. "Pria?" Her fresh tears were answer enough. "Is it safe here?"

"For now. Yes."

Shin moved her back into the basement hallway and closed the door behind him. "Did you put the chains on the doors?"

"No. No. They kept Pria from escaping."

At the soft sound of their voices something moved within the root cellar, pushing against the wooden door with a moan.

"We can't stay here." Maya pointed at the closed elevator doors. "Pria thought I should try to get to the fourth floor through the elevator shaft."

"Why the fourth floor?"

"We have an emergency room there. To shelter in place." Maya turned away, keeping her eyes on the floor. "It's got food and water and stuff." She paused. "And my pictures."

Shin realized that Maya and Pria were the ones who had been taking the food from the pantry. In truth he couldn't fault them. He had his own ration of MREs in his suite back in Hadfield Hall. "Here's the choice for tonight. We leave here and go to Hadfield in the dark. Or we try to get up to the fourth floor to spend the night."

"Are there zombies outside?"

"I don't know."

"Maybe we shouldn't move around in the dark."

Shin nodded. "That's what I was thinking. I can go outside to the escape ladder and climb to the top of the building, let myself in, secure the fourth floor, then come get you."

Maya shook her head. "Please, please don't leave me alone. Please Shin."

He considered her, seeing her panicked eyes and frantic need. "All right. But you do what I say."

"I will. I swear!"

"That means I'm going to need to leave you on the roof while I secure the fourth floor."

Maya nodded. "Okay."

Shin listened to the sound of Pria slapping her hands against the wood and understood Maya's want to leave this place. "Let's go."

The next fifteen minutes were tense ones but, ultimately, safe ones. They both made it to the top of the building where Shin left Maya. He let himself in through the roof access and directly into the fourth floor. A quick search told him the zombies hadn't made it this far and he locked the doors at either end before he retrieved his ward.

When he saw the emergency shelter Maya and Pria had put together he understood why Maya chose to stay here for the night. The two of them would be safe, fed, and comfortable until he figured out what to do next.

* * *

To whom it may concern,

Please consider these to be my last words. Take it as confession or suicide letter. At this point it no longer matters. I am my own judge, jury, and executioner. Sentence to be carried out immediately.

I have done so many bad things in the name of protecting the Salton Academy and its surviving denizens. I was afraid. In the end I couldn't protect the campus or its students from anything or anyone, including myself. My sins are too numerous to mention.

I want those on the supply run to know I'm sorry for what I said. They know what I did. It is their choice to reveal it or not. But, I am truly, honestly, sorry.

In this envelope are keys to the Commons and to the pantry in the kitchen. The pantry is locked. My last act is to make certain the remaining food is safe for whomever is left alive. There are about three months of food left for fifteen people or less. I left the rustic cookbook I've been using in the pantry as well. It shows how to make all sorts of food from the staples that are there.

I hope whoever finds this can use what is there.

Sincerely,
Jeff Meadows

Shin pocketed the keys then folded the letter and considered it before adding it to the pocket with the keys. Following a hunch, he left the Commons and traced the single track of steps that lead from the front of the Commons to the back of it. There he found a ladder on the ground next to one of the large closed trash bins.

He eyed steps to the trash bin, then righted the ladder and climbed until he could lift the lid and look inside. In the kindness of the early morning light Jeff could have been sleeping. He was half-bundled up in a sleeping bag in one corner of the trash bin. Only the exposed arm with the needle sticking out of it told Shin what had happened.

After Jeff had written the letter he had killed himself with a drug overdose. But, ever the neat boy, the youngest Eagle Scout in the tri-cities area, Jeff had decided to dispose of his body at the same time. Shin didn't bother to get close enough to see what the drug was. What mattered was that Jeff was dead. One more student Shin had failed to protect.

Shin bowed his head and murmured a prayer for Jeff's soul before he closed the trash bin and decided what to tell Maya of the boy who had locked her in with a building full of zombies.

In the meantime, the Commons would become their new home. It had food, the water pump, and the wood stove. It was what they needed. At least for now."

CHAPTER
SIXTEEN

Three months later...

J oe and Nicholas approached the side door in the stone wall
of the Salton Academy with excitement and trepidation. They
saw a clear plastic bag attached to the door. There was a white
envelope in it. As Joe pulled it from the door, the door swung
in, admitting them. The teens gave each other a worried glance.

"We should read this now," Joe said as they stepped through
the wall and onto Salton Academy property.

"Yeah." Nicholas closed the door behind him, keeping a
watch out for the worse.

Joe scanned the letter. "Oh boy. Listen to this: "*Dear Lee,
Melissa, Joe, and Nicolas. The academy was overrun with zombies. The
why and how of it can be explained when we meet. Bonny Hall and*

the gymnasium are filled with zombies and are locked up. Do not go near either building. The only survivors are myself, Shin Yoshida, and Maya Chand. We are currently living in the Commons. If we are not there we will be in Hadfield Hall. Come to the Commons and wait for us, please. We have much to talk about. I know this is a poor greeting but welcome home. Sincerely, Shin."

"I know what we're doing." Nicholas looked toward the Commons.

"Inviting them to come home with us. There's room and… God. Poor Maya and Shin."

Joe and Nicholas walked toward the Commons. The walk became a run as Maya and Shin came out to meet them.

ABOUT THE
AUTHOR

Jennifer Brozek is a Hugo Award-nominated editor and an award-winning author. Winner of the Australian Shadows Award for best edited publication, Jennifer has edited fifteen anthologies with more on the way, including the acclaimed *Chicks Dig Gaming* and *Shattered Shields* anthologies. Author of *Apocalypse Girl Dreaming, Industry Talk*, the *Karen Wilson Chronicles*, and the *Melissa Allen* series, she has more than sixty-five published short stories, and is the Creative Director of Apocalypse Ink Productions.

Jennifer is a freelance author for numerous RPG companies. Winner of the Scribe, Origins, and ENnie awards, her contributions to RPG sourcebooks include *Dragonlance, Colonial Gothic, Shadowrun, Serenity, Savage Worlds*, and *White Wolf SAS*. Jennifer is the author of the award winning YA *Battletech* novel,

The Nellus Academy Incident, and *Shadowrun* novella, *Doc Wagon 19.* She has also written for the AAA MMO *Aion* and the award winning videogame, *Shadowrun Returns.*

When she is not writing her heart out, she is gallivanting around the Pacific Northwest in its wonderfully mercurial weather. Jennifer is a Director-at-Large of SFWA, and an active member of HWA and IAMTW. Read more about her at www. jenniferbrozek.com or follow her on Twitter at @JenniferBrozek.